ELROY NIGHTS

ELROY NIGHTS

FREDERICK BARTHELME

COUNTERPOINT

A MEMBER OF THE PERSEUS BOOKS GROUP

NEW YORK

Published by Counterpoint,
A Member of the Perseus Books Group

Counterpoint books are available at special discounts for bulk purchases in the United
States by corporations, institutions, and other organizations. For more information,
please contact the Special Markets Department at the Perseus Books Group, 11 Cambridge Center, Cambridge MA 02142, or call (617) 252-5298, (800) 255-1514 or
e-mail j.mccrary@perseusbooks.com.

Designed by Jeff Williams

Library of Congress Cataloging-in-Publication Data
Barthelme, Frederick, 1943–
    Elroy Nights / Frederick Barthelme.
        ISBN 1–58243–128–0 (alk. paper)
        I. Title.
PS3552.A763E47 2003
813'.54—dc21   2003007830

03 04 05 / 10 9 8 7 6 5 4 3 2 1

for Rie & Katheryn

1

———

Clare and I had been having some disagreements, some dif-
ferences of opinion, not a lot, but enough so that things
between us were up in the air, and we had talked about separating, the way people will, casually, as if it were a step we might
take to sort of improve things, to get some space into the marriage, some room to maneuver. Neither of us had big plans; we'd
just gotten to the point where we were wondering how we got
where we were, why we stayed. With everything else going on—
terrorists, war, guys with nine-year-olds buried in their back-
yards—our problems seemed *slight,* even to us. But they were
ours, which counted for something. We lived on the water in
D'Iberville, Mississippi, and things seemed strained; there wasn't
any life and death reason we had to be in the same house, under
the same roof.

That house was an older brick thing surrounded by palms, mossy oaks, and a powerfully green lawn, back off the road, bathed in deep shadows. On one side was a trellised walk that led to a carriage house with a stone patio and a small pond for carp. Don't ask—it came with the property. On the other side was an acre and a half of overgrowth. Behind us was Back Bay Biloxi, an inlet from the Mississippi Sound that looped in behind the peninsula, maybe a mile wide right behind the house, directly across from Keesler Air Force Base. Relaxing on the deck you sometimes saw a couple of jets scoot up out of nowhere and roar off due south over the Gulf. The water was surprisingly clean and pretty, dotted with islands of marsh grass; tall birds with four-foot wingspans flew around out there as if scheduled by the art director. They'd stand by the shore in the water, on one foot or two, dip their long beaks into the mud, then straighten up and stare around as if checking to be certain they were being watched.

Clare's daughter, Winter, had lived with us until recently. I'd always liked Winter, right through grade school and high school, though she was loud like a cherry bomb, like a whole bag of cherry bombs, which wore on me. When she was in high school, we'd been disappointed as her girlfriends became seedier and duller—I was more disappointed than Clare, who figured it would pass. Winter got into some trouble with a guy named Noble Furlong, who owned a bar over in Waveland, on the far western end of the Mississippi coast. It was nothing big, but it had us scared for a while. We never did get the details—she was a close-mouthed child who went off on you if you pressed her. Maybe we had pandered overmuch during the binge drinking phase, or the "borrowed" car phase, or the "stay out all night with a girlfriend" phase. Anyway, Winter seemed to get in and out of trouble with regularity and dexterity, and after a while we worried less. Turns out kids are resilient.

When Winter hit eighteen she moved out, got an apartment with one of her dodgier friends, and left us at the house with the dog, Wavy, who followed Clare wherever she went. Clare and I didn't adjust very well to being alone with each other. In a matter of months, Clare was sleeping in one of the upstairs bedrooms, and after a year or so she had moved all her clothes and makeup and books—pretty much everything personal—into the bedroom up there. And soon after that, every night when she went to bed I felt a little bit relieved to have the downstairs to myself.

The house was quiet without Winter. You could hear the birds outside, the water running in the pipes when we watered in the summer evenings, the reassuring click of the air conditioning firing up. There were times when the house felt like a library. Moving through it at midnight, with Clare already asleep, I took pleasure in the swish of steps on carpet, the whine of the fan in the desktop computer, the creak of the plywood subflooring, the occasional *smack!* of a bird flying to the light and hitting our clerestory windows.

Clare and I weren't used to spending so much time together. We scrambled for things to do. We sat outside on the deck, walked over to the carriage house, talked about cleaning it out for a studio, counted the carp circling in the pond there. We watched TV news and made fun of the announcers, stared blankly at the news itself, the confrontational stuff, the shouted stuff, the Palestinians and Israelis, the out-of-control U.S. propaganda, the mind-numbing news announcers filling the air with babble. Afghanistan, Iraq, intrepid reporters with their artfully turned up collars. We dialed through the channels, spending altogether too much time on forensics and house shows and Court TV, where we found the usual array of tabloid stories. We listened intently to Robert Blake, to the embarrassingly media-hungry Ed Smart, to Dan Rather speaking so softly. We followed the TV folk, a tattered lot, parroting each other on the air. These TV people were our closest friends.

After a bit we talked about us. At first it was delicate and unrevealing, but as days wore on we became a little more forthcoming, not always a good thing. We expressed our affection in timid ways, we talked about how we might feel if we lived in separate places. This idea had come up before in our marriage. It wasn't anger or eagerness to taste the forbidden, it was not boredom or distaste, it wasn't that nagging horror of the companion whose every utterance rakes your nerves raw, it wasn't the test your love theory of marriage, the trial separation, or the primacy of personal space. Clare and I were still together, fond of each other, devoted. The idea of living apart was simply a formalizing of the distance at which we preferred to be, the comfortable distance.

In the middle of October I leased a condo on the beach in east Biloxi, between downtown and the casino row at the end of the peninsula. It was called Windswept—a pair of stepped buildings with their backs facing each other, like a seven-story pyramid pulled apart around an open court. There was fancy glass and steel business spanning the opening at the top. The front units faced the Gulf of Mexico, each condo jutting out under the unit above, like giant steps from the seventh floor to the carefully landscaped grounds. I got a lease-purchase on a clean front unit and hired some art students from the university where I taught to move a few pieces of furniture from the house.

Clare came over to help at first, and it was pleasant being there with her in this new place. But I also knew she wasn't going to stay. We messed with the furniture, moved it around. There was so little of it that you could put it anywhere, and it still looked as if it was stored in an empty apartment. I liked that. Clare and I had a kind of stilted sex for the first time in ages, and it was as if we were strangers—self-conscious, embarrassing, but nasty the way those things sometimes go. It had been so long we didn't have a clue. That wasn't such a big success.

We met one of my neighbors, who turned out to be Mrs. Eleanor Scree, a woman we'd known years before when we first came to the coast; she and her husband had managed the apartment project we'd lived in then. At Windswept she was the resident manager. She showed condominiums, handled summer rentals and sublets, and worked with the grounds people—as ever.

Winter turned up in D'Iberville, so Clare took the opportunity to wish me good luck and went back to the house. I was left to do my late nights at the Windswept condo, looking out into the pretty Gulf.

2

Apart from a couple of calls, I didn't hear from Clare for nearly a month. Then she invited me for dinner with Winter and some new girlfriend of Winter's named Freddie. "This girl's in your class or something," Clare said on the phone. "Or *going* to be in your class. I don't know."

"Beats me," I said. "Do I need to bring anything?"

"Just your condo-bound self," she said.

Later that afternoon, as I drove across the bridge from Biloxi to D'Iberville, I thought how we'd started as young people insisting on living the way we wanted, and how we'd gradually retreated from that, from doing what we wanted. Things change. What you want becomes something you can't imagine having wanted, and instead you have *this*, suddenly and startlingly not at all what you sought. One day you find yourself walking around in

Ralph Lauren shorts and Cole Haan loafers and no socks. You're wearing an Eddie Bauer T-shirt and a wristwatch that cost as much as your first car. You think, How did this happen? It isn't a terrible spot, and you don't feel bad about being there, being the person you are, in the place you are, with the wife or husband you have, the stepdaughter, the friends and acquaintances, the house and tools and toys, the job, but there is no turning back. You have a Daytimer full of things to do. You have a Palm PDA and names and addresses and contacts, and there is no way back. Even if there were a way back, you couldn't get there from here, and you probably wouldn't go if you could. The effort required isn't the kind of effort you can make anymore.

———

Winter said, "I'm Rocky and Bullwinkle." She shook my hand stiffly. "Those aren't my real names," she said.

"I guessed that," I said.

"I was trying to remember the *Rocky and Bullwinkle Show,* and I just thought it would be cool to be Rocky *and* Bullwinkle. One of them was a moose."

"But you want to be both of them?" I said.

"I'm making a new persona for myself," she said. "It's like a performance piece. Or I was thinking of Winter Muntz. You ever hear of Mad Man Muntz? Retail czar? He was my real dad's brother or something, uncle maybe. Sold TVs and cars in Texas in the fifties. Everything pink." She pointed to her friend. "This is Freddie."

"Hello, Freddie," I said, holding the hand Freddie held out for me to hold. "How are you?"

"Good," Freddie said. "I know some of your students—Heidi and Edward Works and some others."

"Edward is one of my best," I said. "You guys are friends?"

"Yeah. I'm taking your 523 in the spring."

"Starting an M.A.?" I said.

"I guess. Starting something. I want to make art."

"Don't we all," I said. "Well, I look forward to seeing your stuff." I turned back to Winter, put my arm around her shoulders. "I like your names, Winter. Every one of them."

She looked different. She was always changing her look anyway, but this new one was kind of dark. Black, you could say. Black hair, cut a little bit dotty-looking, the whole presentation something in the Popeye way, though I guess Popeye only had the three hairs, so she was sort of fertile Popeye, hairwise. She clearly knew she had some kind of deal going, and she splashed the makeup around to show it off. She had always been pretty.

"Freddie needs a place to stay for a few weeks," Winter said, curled on the floor of the dining room with the dog. "Her house is being fixed."

"Oh," Freddie said. "I can go stay with Furlong." She needled her hair with a ballpoint.

"Furlong?" I said, looking to Clare. "Same Furlong?"

"Don't sweat it," Winter said.

"Well, we can talk about that," Clare said, shaking her head. "What happened to your house?"

"Somebody went through the floor," Freddie said. "It's a twenties place, wood floors, weak, rotted, some guy was doing an in-place somersault and he made it, but he went right through. So the landlord is taking this opportunity to make lots of fix-ups. I think he's trying to sell or something. Landlords will do that to you."

"Let's watch TV," Winter said, getting off the floor where she'd been strangle-petting Wavy. She led Freddie back to her bedroom. "Call us, O.K., Mom? When it's ready?"

When the door shut, I said, "Uh-huh. She's fine. A step up for Winter's friends."

"Looks a little *Road Warrior* to me."

"Well, that's still a look. I see it at school. It gives them that world-weariness that we worked so hard to acquire."

"Oh, he's cynical," Clare said, slipping her eyes my way. "He's still cynical."

"Am not. If she's a friend of Edward's, she's probably O.K. He's a good kid, works hard—some of his stuff is pretty interesting, videos and such. She's probably O.K."

I stretched out on the sofa with Wavy. He was content to stay with me as long as I was petting him with vigor and imagination. Otherwise, no. The living room had a high ceiling and a half-dozen windows that overlooked the bay. A deck spanned the back of the house. There was a once-used Jacuzzi out there, now a site for potted plants. Up close to the house the deck overlooked a low brick-walled courtyard with much high-quality landscaping. We didn't do the landscaping ourselves; we hired it—Treetop Lawn and Garden. It was an entry every month in the joint checking account, two hundred dollars. Plus supplies and equipment.

Wavy was showing me his teeth. His tongue twisted out of the side of his upside-down mouth, falling down now over the top of his muzzle. He watched me from this vantage as I petted the underside of his chin, scratched his ears in circles, dragged my fingers through his chest hair. He put his front feet on my chest and kept me at leg's length. I wondered if that was because at that distance he could focus better or if it was some other dog idea I'd never get.

Clare stepped around the kitchen island holding her wine glass. She wore legging-tight jeans and an oxford cloth shirt. She looked fresh and well-to-do. "You're not worried?" she said.

"Not yet," I said. "You're a handsome woman, Clare. So striking."

"Why, thank you very much. My husband used to tell me that."

"You crispy," I said.

She smiled. "I guess that could mean many things."

"It does," I said. "It absolutely does."

She looked distracted, so I said, "I don't see a problem here. I mean with Winter and what's her name. You're letting them stay, right? Might be fun for a while. They might turn out to be lovely." Wavy rolled off his back, got to his feet, scurried up the sofa and dived off, and clicked across the floor to Clare. There he tumped over on his side, his head backwards, looking at her upside down, just as he'd been looking at me moments before.

"Quit," she said. "Put your head down."

Wavy did as he was told.

———

I'd taught art for years at Dry River Community College. Then, when the community college became a certified four-year school, we became Dry River University. After a few years, we added a couple of M.A. programs, one in art. I taught a little of everything, but it had come down to painting and drawing, which was fine with me because I was sort of qualified to teach that. I'd studied painting in college, taken my M.F.A, had plenty of local shows, been in a few national shows. But my life as an artist did not last nearly long enough, and while I sold lots of drawings and small paintings over the years, the demand was not high. I gradually lost interest in myself, the things I made, and in the trouble I had to go to in order to be an artist. Making pictures was the easy part. Hard was the posturing, the self-presentation—you just get tired after a while, and once you realize that you are not Braque, what is the point?

People are scared of artists, still haven't a clue about them. This was true when I was in college, and it's true now. It may even be truer now, because the students these days take a lot for granted—they'll tie a cow to a refrigerator and want to put it in the college gallery. I explain that I like the idea, that it's a great idea, but would they consider something not so . . . *alive?*

No. The guy in NY "did" an elephant.

So I got less interested in myself, in "my art," which by mid-life could not escape the quotation marks, and I turned my attention to the students, who I found saving. They were always fascinating, interesting, and odd. They had queer belief systems and were not much at all like the dopey kids on TV. That is, they shared the talk and the dress and the gestures, but they were complicated and sensitive and more genuine than I would have imagined it was possible for a young person to be now. I liked their ideas, I liked living their lives with them, I liked advise and consent, so I stayed put at Dry River, and in the fullness of time, moved up to the exalted post of Professor of Art.

The university was parked on an oak-strewn plot across from the beach on the Coast Highway. It was not a good school. Among the faculty there were interesting and pleasant people and others not so interesting, but all of us passionately explained why we produced so little actual work, the explanation wrapped in our best cultural studies jargon, naturally. At our worst, we were rainy-day children in grandma's scented clothes, our smooth faces smeared with gobs of taillight-red lipstick and wild sweeps of eye shadow, our puffy chests adorned with strings of low-hanging pearls. We played. In short, par for the course.

The students had an accurate picture of us—the last limp hurdles they had to clear before they were allowed out into *the world itself.* We held the fort, and they wanted it, or more correctly, they wanted to get through it and out of town. We were proactive and student centered, and we herded them through our programs with enthusiasm and astonishing speed—they were Monopoly money. A careful observer might have wondered about our standards, but we assured ourselves in great and lengthy faculty meetings that we were at one with the current thinking in education, thinking that, in most cases, derived from that "take thy bond and write eighty" thing Jesus did so long ago.

While we were at it, and in the tradition of colleges and universities everywhere, we had our fair share of uses for the students: pawns, trophies, toys, targets, children, pets, lovers, even instructors. By and large, the students took this in stride. They had, after all, been students all their lives and knew what to expect. We were old, and we did not matter.

From my view we were sort of dead already. Excepting, of course, those few among us who thought instead that they were still a part of the discussion, the ongoing negotiation of what the world was, or was to become. These individuals bought themselves dark, racy clothes, hung out with the children, did their drugs, went to their parties, danced all night, tried eagerly to take off the years. Me, I was a go-home guy. I put in an appearance, Clare on my arm, ate lightly from the buffet, left at nine. After fifteen years of this, I had a nice little job that required not so much work and paid well enough, in the university way.

———

At dinner Clare asked Freddie where she was from, and Freddie said she was a runaway, a long-time street person who got out of the life, member in good standing of some new generation I didn't catch the name of. Not completely without irony, I told her I was a member of the Love Generation, and, when she said that was cool, I went on to tell her I'd been at Woodstock, Altamont, and in the Haight in the day.

"He was nine," Clare said.

"Was not," I said. "I was sixteen. The dog is named after Ken Kesey's bus driver."

"Nope," Clare said.

Then I told Freddie and Winter about my days with Country Joe McDonald.

"Who?" Winter said.

"Never mind," I said.

Winter said, "Listen, you really have to hear Freddie's story. It's awful."

"It was great," Freddie said. "What are you talking about?"

"Abandoned as a child," Winter said. "Then, adopted and returned several times to a state facility in New Mexico, and finally taken by a couple in Santa Fe."

"You're telling her story?" I said to Winter.

"It was fine," Freddie said. "Quit." She gave Winter a little slap on the shoulder.

"This couple was childless, and they treated her like a dog. She was like a toy, this little person they could wind up and make obey them."

"They *were* high on obedience," Freddie said, her fork poised like a pencil over the pork chop Clare had prepared. "That is true."

"Well, no wonder she took off, right? Fifteen going on fifty," Winter said. "Everybody said that about her—social workers, truckers, drunks in bars, losers in hotels. Right, Freddie?"

Freddie nodded, but when Winter turned back to us, Freddie gave a little shake of her head as if to say, *Not really*. I recognized the Eddie Izzard joke.

"So tell the story," Winter said.

"Another time," Freddie said. "Was nothing, was long ago and far away."

"Her actual real parents got shot in a convenience store robbery when she was eleven. They ran the place, her mama did—her daddy was the janitor. They were shot by Mexicans. These Mexicans came in one night—"

"With their skinny little moustaches," Freddie said, grinning.

"Really!" Winter said. "They started poking their guns around, and one went off, then another, and pretty soon they had a shoot-out. Two minutes more and the Mexicans were flying out of the joint in a starlite-blue Pontiac Bonneville, leaving her mama and daddy on the floor bleeding."

"That's bad," Clare said.

"It was bad," Winter said. She went after her pork chop with a heavy fist on the knife handle.

"So what happened then?" Clare said to Freddie.

"Don't worry," Winter said, sprawling over a couple of chairs on her side of the table. "The parents live."

"I had to take care of Daddy," Freddie said.

"After a while her mama got jealous—no reason for it but some people are just that way—and shot him in the forehead with this gun they got after the robbery. Pop! Just like that."

"Jesus," I said.

"I was amazed how little the hole was where the bullet entered his skull," Freddie said. "It was real little." She made a hole with her thumb and forefinger.

"After that she stayed at her grandmother's in El Paso, but when she hit high school she was toast, ended up a year in some place called the Certification School for Troubled Kids."

"Youth," Freddie said. "Troubled Youth."

"Right," Winter said. "So she busted out."

"Not really," Freddie said. "I left on a bus."

"Quite a story," I said.

"It was ages ago," Freddie said. "I'm all settled down now. Into my college years."

"See that, Winter?" Clare said. "Freddie's settled down, and she's not much older than you."

I got up and started clearing the table.

"So who was this Furlong person Winter was living with in Waveland?" Clare said to Freddie. "Friend of yours?"

"Oh, Mom. Forget it, will you? Why do you have to bring that up?" Winter said. "Just this guy. His name's Noble Furlong, and I wasn't really living with him in the way you're saying it. He owns a club there, the Kit Kat Klub. He's like forty-something, like your age, you know? But he was like real nice to me. Gave me money and stuff. He looked kind of beat up, but he was nice. I did some work for him, you know? Cleaning and stuff. He took me out riding in his Cadillac and told me he was stung with my great pubescent beauty."

Clare froze and did a squinty stare.

"Yeah, I know," Winter said.

"We all went out there one night," Freddie said. "A lot of the kids at the college hang out there. It's a great place. Peach-colored, just back off the beach. He stopped in the middle of the highway at three in the morning and showed us. Asked us how we liked it. Said we could all live there together if we wanted."

"He has a heart of gold," I said.

"Well, I was planning on being mean as a switch," Freddie said. "But Poochie had other ideas."

"Did not," Winter said.

"Like the time he asked you how you felt about him?" Freddie said.

"I told him, 'You know, Furlong, I love you for the man you want to be, and I love you for the man you almost are,' which he found so heartbreaking that he busted into tears," Winter said. "I guess he didn't see the movie."

"He's kind of harmless," Freddie said. "The best part was going across the street at night, finding that string of lights looped along the front of his stupid club, wind slicing across the highway, the Gulf running in and out in the dark. Sometimes I'd stand out in the middle of that highway for hours at a time, just so I could feel the weather."

"She loves weather," Winter said.

"But then her pal had to declare his love," Freddie said. "Man, there is nothing I hate more than some hopeless creep declaring his love. I mean, keep it to yourself."

"Amen in a bottle," Winter said.

"So when he finally gets down to it," Freddie said, "he tells her how much he loves her and how much he needs her and how much he wants to be her friend and make an honest woman out of her, and she tells him that she is already just about twice as honest a woman as he will ever want to meet."

"And that's a big adios," Winter said.

"In a bottle," I said.

"That's it," Winter said. "You got it. And that's the story of how we ended up here at home today."

Clare nodded, going very cool. She seemed a little off center. "So, Freddie—you're in school full time?"

"She's an art major," Winter said. "We told you that, didn't we? And she talked me into starting again, too. Maybe in the summer. Sometimes I go to classes with her, but I'm taking a semester off right now."

"Right," Clare said. "You're going to be in Elroy's class. What's the report on him, anyway?"

Freddie laughed. "I hear he's creepy but helpful," she said. "I really need to try this, so I guess he'll be good for me. I like school. I'm ready to get started."

"I like three-D concept-based action painting," Winter said. "Or whatever. Performance art, DVD stuff. Sequential art. You name it. I guess I'm just into trying different things now."

"So, you're starting, too?" I said. "Art department? A new major?"

"Summer," she said. "Not until summer. I was just going to try it, don't you know? Whatever. You think I shouldn't? You don't think I can? I mean, you're an artist, right? Dad?"

———

The girls left when we weren't quite through with dinner. Clare and I stayed at the table and ate in silence, smiled at each other from time to time.

She got up to clear the table. I got up to help her. She said, "I've heard a lot about Freddie, but this is the first I've met her. She needs to stay a while, then they maybe live together."

"She seems fine to me. Pretty. Could be worse," I said.

"Pretty," Clare said. "I like that. You want coffee?"

I cleared the rest of the table, stacking the dishes as I'd done for years. In a few minutes the coffee was hopping, Clare had the dishes rinsed and into the dishwasher, and I had the coffee cups on a tray. "You think it's too chilly for outside?" I said.

"It's fine," she said.

We settled on the deck looking out over the silvery green still water between Biloxi and our part of D'Iberville. Clare sighed. "I'm not sure I've done a good job. With her, you, anything," she said.

"She's fine," I said. "You think we did better before? I think she's fine. The story wasn't all that bad. I'm not happy about Furlong, though."

"He's nothing," she said. "Besides, Winter's always hanging out with strange people."

"Yeah," I said. "Fond of gruesome. Still, fingers and toes."

Clare said, "The thing is, you want her to stay here, go to college, go to law school, marry a doctor, start a practice defending the rights of whales."

"Agreed," I said. A small breeze slipped past us.

It was pleasant at the house with Clare. I liked her more, remembered how I trusted all her gestures, how funny she was in an off, private way. She was lovelier than ever. I was wondering about that, thinking how a face becomes sort of generic if you see it too much, and how it pops back into focus sometimes, surprising you.

She said, "I don't mind this arrangement, do you? Living alone? Has its virtues. Do you find that?"

I thought I might try and figure if that was a trick question, but then I realized she would see right through me, so I said, "I sort of do. I guess."

She said, "I miss you, but I like it, too. It's awfully quiet most of the time. Winter's in and out, and I'm here alone. I have a much more powerful sense of the place—trees, water, the whole thing. It's very restful. It's like listening to rain or trains in the night. I didn't have so much of that when I was worried all the time."

"When I was here?" I said.

"Yeah. What you were doing, what we were doing. It's cleaner this way. Not caring is much nastier than anger, isn't it? Sometimes I wish we were at each other's throats."

"That'd be easier," I said. "Maybe we're just full of self-loathing."

"Oh, that's good," Clare said. "TV?"

"Yeah. Sorry. I was just looking around for some slag to put in this hole in the conversation here, and it arrived."

"Well, look elsewhere, will you? Look harder."

I waved my agreement to another cup of coffee, and Clare collected the cups and went inside. I took the time to look at my ex-backyard, my ex-vista. Didn't seem the same. I was visiting somebody. The view was mine and not mine at the same moment. I knew every detail, the line of the weeds along the bay, the blackened pilings, the slumped pier that jutted out at the back of the property, the little island in the bay with the tall swaying grasses, the casino that stood straight and tall east of the bridge from D'Iberville into Biloxi. Clare and I had spent long late afternoons on the deck in spring and early summer, when it was cool enough, and then again into the fall, and I wanted to do that again, to sit there with her and listen to the cars, the crickets, the locusts, the ducks, the gulls, to smell the water, feel the breeze, soak it all up. What was stopping me?

"How's Mrs. Scree?" Clare said, coming back outside. "Still watching over you?"

"Like a hawk," I said. "She on your payroll?"

Clare laughed. "Of course she is. Like all the young attractive women I manage to shanghai for you. All spies. All working for me."

"I'm flattered," I said. "But I can't figure what it is you want to know."

"I will never tell," Clare said, patting the back of my hand.

We sat out there for another half hour or so, talking occasionally, worrying about Winter together, but also just sitting, relaxing, enjoying the place, the feel of it—the air, the sharp scent of late fall. It was a little chilly, but not so much to scare us inside. There were evening birds, there was water lapping against the shore.

Finally, I said, "I think I'd better go. I could get used to this."

"Were," she said.

"Could be again."

"Well, you're always welcome," she said. "It's nice out here, don't you think? Come when you want to. When you get tired of the view from the condo, just come over and use the deck. You are welcome anytime."

"Watch out or I'll be here in the middle of the night."

"Just don't wake me," she laughed.

She walked me to the car and stood in the drive as I pulled out. I wondered if she was lonely, if I was lonely, but by the time I hit the bridge I was glad to be moving, glad to be riding through the night with the wind coming in the windows, glad that the bills were paid and Clare didn't hate me too much, looking forward to being home with the door locked and the lights barely on, going though my routine in pristine, undisturbed privacy.

3

The condo overlooked the harbor of Biloxi and Deer Island, less than a mile away, a spit of land only a hundred fifty or two hundred yards wide at its widest point, riddled with pines. Closer to me were the casinos, just east and just west of downtown. Biloxi used to be a pleasantly seedy bayside place where nobody had any money, and it didn't matter that nobody had any money. Everybody got suntanned, then sunburned, then roasted, and by the middle of July the restaurants were full of turkey-brown people raking over plates of fish, shrimp, oysters, tomatoes, potatoes—anything that could be fried.

It had been a lovely town in that down-at-the-heels way, as sandy and serene as any town of its kind ever was. Then came the casinos, with promises and buildings and jobs, and the state bit hard, letting the gaming commission write its own gambling laws, passing them as quickly as they were written. The town changed. Where it used to be seedy in a quaint fifties way, it was now up-to-the-minute garish—the usual pink buildings, casinos shaped like pirate ships, miles of bend-it-yourself neon. Biloxi's thugs had often been prominent citizens—mayors who had people killed for cash flow, folks connected to the Southern mafia, people for whom embezzlement was a princely routine. Those plus the henchmen, the hulking and ignorant guys roughing up people in that *film noir* way. Gambling changed all that. The roughing up got quieter and legal. No trouble ever came to light except when a couple of Vietnamese shot each other at five in the morning in some dew-covered casino parking lot, and mostly that got passed off in the paper as that hot Asian temper you'd heard so much about, just coincidently gone off near the Boomtown or the Caravaggio. When you saw casino people, they were decked out in Armani, at lunch in one of their restaurants with politicians who tended to grovel openly. Armani looked a little out of place on the Mississippi coast, so you noticed. Maybe we'd gotten a little bit of an Atlantic City or Vegas look in our political world, a new kind of swarthy you can't get on fishing boats.

I spent a lot of nights not quite believing I was living alone, walking around in a body that seemed awkward, a sagging thing that had begun to look like the older men I saw at the beach. When I crossed the street for a walk in the sand the girls in their beach gear passed me without the slightest glance, or if they noticed, it was, "Are you O.K.?" as if they were ready to stop their party and drive me to the hospital in their bikinis if necessary. Same thing in the halls at school, and in elevators, grocery stores. When this unhappy deference began, I couldn't pinpoint, but it hadn't been going on for years or I would have noticed.

I called Clare more often than she called me, and she was patient, just like always. But most of the time I was O.K. What I liked about living alone there on the seventh floor was that nothing ever changed. The living room was always perfectly straightened. The couch and chairs well plumped. The magazines on the coffee table were always current, the fireplace spotless. The dining room was spare, mostly a kind of office space where my computer and I sat during the late nights. Everything was stacked around in neat piles. My bedroom was pristine, my closet orderly. My kitchen was right out of a model home. From the moment I got up in the morning to when I went to bed at night, I was surrounded by order, by a pervasive *cleanness,* by a kind of propriety that I found comforting, satisfying, even touching. Maybe it was melancholy. But I liked the way the light marched across the room during the day, streaming through the wide floor-to-ceiling glass that led out onto my shallow balcony overlooking the Gulf. I liked the look of the too-expensive outdoor furniture, carefully dotted out there. I liked to watch the fireworks of sunsets, which I could see down to my right, and sunrises, which I caught off to my left sometimes on my way to bed for the day. I liked the click of my heels on the tile in the entry and the kitchen.

I'd always been fond of that machine-for-living thing, that *it cleans itself!* world, and that's what the condo was. Locked up in it, I felt I was in some kind of vacuum-packed container. A package on a shelf in some giant grocery, with giant people occasionally leaning down to check my freshness date, now long past. I imagined them from time to time, big eyes in my windows. I didn't want to invite anyone to live there with me, though Clare was always welcome; there was enough space, two bedrooms, two baths, good high ceilings—but it seemed a one-person craft. Another human around would mess things up. I was particularly fond of the heavy carpet I'd had installed. It was a perfect neutral color, and it never got disturbed. Footprints didn't show on it. It never looked walked on or used. I wasn't sure how they managed that. I'd read about it in a magazine, asked for it at the floor store, and it was supplied.

Then I forgot what kind of carpet it was. Forgetting was a mainstay of my act, and I didn't mind. Well, I'd gotten used to it. When talking with people, I liked to wiggle my hand in circles as though I were trying to remember, wave to the person to whom I was talking so that he or she might supply the name, the word I was seeking. People are amazingly good at that, and I am grateful.

I did not think I'd be one for the quiet life, but it turned out I liked it rather much. My days were sleepy—I was usually up all night, going to bed around five or six in the morning. At night I read magazines, worked on photographs, watched DVDs or television—all-night programming, infomercials for products that increased penis size, breast size, booty size, for products that increased sexual stamina, removed or grew hair, made people smell better to others, taught you how to make a fortune buying and selling cars or real estate or by placing tiny classified ads in hundreds of newspapers all around the nation. I was always working at the computer, doing menial tasks—reorganizing files, erasing old files, backing up particular sets of files, reading news groups, writing e-mails, downloading new programs, studying the file lists, entering dialogues in news groups, buying software that I could download immediately. I worked on a new iMac, along with an older PC, and often I was still awake at first light. When the time came, I left the computers running but shut everything else down, snapped off all the lights in the house, started the dishwasher, and went into my bedroom where I opened the windows for a while. I stretched out on the bed, and I listened to the sounds outside—the cars that went by on the beach highway, the water, the night birds and crickets, the trains in the distance, small planes overhead, the city police sirens, our air conditioning compressors, the howl of four-wheel-drive vehicles speeding down the road, the squabbling ducks that sometimes settled in the small pond in front of the condominium building. The ringing in my ears of so much silence. When I was ready to sleep, I shut the sliding doors and pulled the curtains, put on a CD out of my collection of home-made digital recordings of other nights—rainstorms, throaty crickets, or just ordinary nights with ordinary night noises—set it to repeat, then undressed and lay on the bed, on the top of the bedspread, pulled the cotton throw over me, and recited childhood prayers—the Our Father and Hail Mary, my favorites—until sleep carried me away.

4

A couple weeks after the dinner at Clare's, I ran into Freddie at the car wash. I was behind her in line at the pumps where you filled up and made arrangements for the kind of wash you wanted. There were a couple of cars in front of us. Freddie had a new feeling about her—chopped up hair and broad shoulders, a good stride. She looked young and handsome in that weathered way women who've had some tough sledding always have, and I was stung by that. I was pretending to do something in the car, but the truth was I was staring hard, like I might do at a photograph of a woman in a magazine.

The car wash was a big outfit that was usually crowded with all the young, happy folk getting their BMWs cleaned a mile a minute, but this day the place was nearly empty. I was in the car behind Freddie, and I was thinking I ought to get out and walk right up to her, reintroduce myself. Then I figured that might be awkward, so I sat there being patient in my car, but I noticed that I was posing a lot. I couldn't help it. I put my hand on the side of my face, and then I sort of felt it there and saw myself in my imagination like some pathetic-looking guy posed in a *GQ* advertisement, maybe in the back of a scene in an ad, so I changed positions, but a minute later the same realization came up again. I could not sit right. I heard the spraying water and the blower of the wash tunnel flipping on and off. Late afternoon light streamed under the aging canopy, throwing long shadows everywhere. I imagined myself at the condo with her, young and pretty and sucking all the oxygen out of the place. I figured my chances were not so good. So I sat and soaked it all in—the evening light, the high, wide translucent cover over the gas pumps, dusty paint flaking off the dirty painted columns beneath it, huge filthy windows in the station off to the right, rusty pipes, and the noise, the incessant noise of the place. Freddie was like some vision. I looked hard. I wasn't subtle.

Alongside the French blue VW, she was a poster girl for grad students—black shirt, white tee underneath, low-slung jeans, skinny sweater, black jacket. She was waiting for the wash girl to take care of her. When she looked my way, I climbed out of the car and said, "Freddie?" loud enough to keep her attention. She was startled, looked at me as if to ask how I knew her name.

It took her a minute to figure out who I was. By that time I was by her side. She was wearing a lot of perfume, something pungent, more of it than was respectable. I figured she knew that.

"Hey," she said, her face brightening. "I remember you. How are you?" She extended her hand.

"Good," I said. I nodded and waved at the few cars in front of us. "Moving slow today."

"Yeah," she said, turning to look.

The girl arranging the wash was a kid of the kind you find working a register at some store and can't figure out why she's there, why she isn't out at the country club where she belongs. Those girls are in classes all the time—perfect skin, perfect hair, big eyes, and wide mouths with perfect rows of handsome teeth. Their mouths are all the same. I've become something of an observer of perfect teeth. This wash girl was stuffed into tiny black jeans and a cowboy shirt, and her hair was all kinds of graceful. She was writing on a tablet she held in her open palm, talking to a big guy in a brown suit with a wide tie splashed with too many stripes. He had bristly hair carefully combed, and he drove a Lincoln sedan, an undertaker's car. He was smitten with her, you could see that. A big friendly man with wad of greasy hair—a repeat customer.

The wash girl patted the man's arm and pointed him toward the waiting room, then slapped a ticket under the windshield wiper of his Lincoln and waved for one of the black guys at the head of the wash tunnel. A tall kid, maybe fourteen, with milk-chocolate dreadlocks, very short and tight, wearing a white jumpsuit, rocked toward her, grinning, whipping his chamois backward and forward, held in two hands, twirling it as if it were a bandanna, his walk a lope, a shuffle, his head a mimicry of those toy dog heads that once bobbed in the back windows of people's cars.

He jumped the Lincoln away.

The attendant came up and introduced herself. "Hi. I'm Nell," she said. "What can we do for you today?"

"Just a wash," Freddie said.

"Both cars, one ticket?" she said, writing something on her ticket, then motioning back and forth between Freddie and me with her pen. "We got a special on. You kids together?"

"You never know," Freddie said.

"Wishes, horses," I said, grinning way too big, caught off guard.

"You want me to do the tires for you?" Nell said, poking Freddie's sidewalls with the shiny metal toe of her cowboy boot.

"*Do* them?" Freddie said.

"Armor All," Nell said. "Two dollars gets you the tires and the whole interior. Another dollar gets you the bumpers."

Freddie stepped back a pace. "Sure," she said. "Let's go all out."

"Wax, too?" Nell said. "A dollar ninety-five."

"Wax," Freddie said.

Nell leaned back and looked at the front of Freddie's car. "I was going to say bug solvent—maybe not."

Freddie said, "Got no bugs."

"You will," Nell said. "It's that time of year. Two-by-two, if you know what I mean. Can't go a mile without coming up covered in 'em."

Freddie turned around and looked at me. "That's a heck of a thing, isn't it? Don't you think?"

I shook my head. "Bugs will be bugs," I said.

Freddie smiled, folded her arms, and waited for Nell to finish her ticket, then headed for the waiting room. I stood around while Nell wrote me up, then took my receipt and went inside. There were just three of us in the glassed-in waiting room, each positioned on our own summery, wrought-iron chair with its print pillow decorated with leaves and limbs. The television across the room was suffering through some late-in-the-day talk. After a minute I dumped my magazine back on the stack and moved closer to Freddie.

She moved slightly away from me, gathering her jacket, smoothing it. "You get your tires done?" she said.

"Rain check," I said. It was startling to be that close to her, to see her eyes so clearly, as if they were a photo blowup, crystal blue and perfectly focused. When she turned I could see the downy hairs on her face. Her lips were fleshy and done up in a few dozen shades of brick.

"How's Winter?" Freddie said.

"Good. You're not staying at the house?"

"No. I'm back at my place. How's Clare?"

"She's good. We're living apart, so I don't see her that much," I said.

"I knew that," she said. "But not really, huh?"

"Sort of," I said.

The burly guy in the suit was wiggling a hand in our direction. Freddie held her arms out to her side. "What?"

"The magazine," the guy said. "Could you hand me the magazine there?"

"This one?" she said, snatching a copy of *Parenting* off the table.

"Thanks," he said, taking it. "I have two—girl twelve, boy nine."

"Well, then, you've got trouble," Freddie said.

The big guy grinned. "No, they're fine. Everybody says it just gets worse and worse and then they move out, but we'll be lucky. Cindy's got her first boyfriend. Had him two years. She cooks for him at our place. It's kind of cute."

Freddie laughed and said, "What're you, like, from Mars or something?"

"Aw, c'mon, don't spoil it for me," he said. Big Fellow rolled his eyes as he flipped the pages of *Parenting,* snapping one after another, left to right. "Maybe we're luckier than I know, huh?"

—————

I had started hanging out with the students in the art department. Clare wasn't around, and there wasn't anyone else to hang out with. I needed to get out, see people, do stuff. I became a regular at their parties, I took them out to dinner, I waded into their lives. It was safe and pleasant. We talked about art all the time, earnestly, at college length. I felt like a kid myself, as if I were back in school. I got close to them in a way I hadn't before, a way

I'd always avoided because I thought it wasn't fair. You don't want to use the job to get friends, coerce people. Besides, being the professor tricked up the game, gave you all these advantages, made for nasty conflicts of interest. So I'd been careful before, but this time I plowed right into them. Pretty soon students were inviting me to dinner, asking me to come to their studios, taking me to the clubs to hear the local bands. I became an indie music expert overnight, dragging out old art rock CDs from when I listened to music, making lists of the greatest bands nobody ever heard of, weaving Cage and Lamont Young, Steve Reich, Robert Ashley into the mix just to keep my credentials.

Talking to the students was refreshing—they had the new world, and everything about it was seductive, renewing. The students were my guides. Students lifted me out of my age, my habits, my troubles. Socializing with them I became the cool professor, the intimate mentor, the guy who could party all night and teach all day. Colleagues who did this routinely were comfortable with the students in a way I had never been—comfortable holding forth, doing private lectures, and later, after drinks and dinner, satisfying themselves with whoever was particularly interested, or particularly drunk, that night. Men and women. Small families grew from these connections. Male students found themselves with surprise children sired on needy female faculty. Women students broke up marriages, wept bitterly at reconciliations.

Outside the classroom I'd always been a guy with a wry smile offering no invitation to intimacy, having nothing to share. Now I needed more from them, and I saw them in a new way, as kids happy to be in their lives, invested in their lives, kids with futures, plans, whole worlds in front of them full of things happening, love and mischief, success, sadness, tragedy. I remembered all that, and I envied them.

In the classroom we could pretend that I was the teacher and they were the students, but out of it, I was inconsequential history. Then things changed. "Dawg," they called me, and I made progress. I became, for a moment, the slightly dangerous professor, the one who dared cross the convention, the one who was always going for coffee or drinks with this attractive student, or that group, the one who went to parties, drank too much, laughed too loud, danced too hard. I knew it was their world. Mine had come and gone, and I hung on only as a feature of their generosity or disinterest. Their ideas had replaced mine; I was harmless and old-fashioned. Time levels everything. One girl explained this to me by saying, "It's the Ricky-Nelson-Was-an-Artist rule."

I bowed to her wisdom.

———

The rest of the fall semester went quickly in this way. Those first months of separation from Clare weren't my favorites, in spite of the new pleasures of students and seclusion. You get apart and then you miss all the stuff that you did together, all the little stuff, the details of a life. I had assumed that we'd get back together, but I did not think it would happen too quickly, because if it did, we would feel as though we'd never separated. But Clare was pissed, too. I didn't get that at first, but after I was out of the house and she didn't call me, or keep up, I got the sense that what had seemed certain was not so certain after all.

We stayed pretty far away from each other all semester. We talked on the phone occasionally, and I went out to the house a couple of times—trying to help with Winter, who was acting up a little. But mostly it was me in the condo and Clare elsewhere. Then, before Christmas, when I hadn't see Clare for most of a month, I heard that Winter was going to Manitoba to stay with friends for the holidays. I called Clare and suggested that we drive the Gulf Coast to the Florida panhandle, then down the west coast to the Keys.

"What about girlfriends?" Clare said.

"Don't have any," I said. "Well—you."

"I'm your fallback?"

After a time I convinced Clare that I wanted to spend Christmas with her, and she agreed to the trip, and we spent a few nights at Seaside, the shabby-but-upscale remake of a quaint Gulf-side town where one of the Hollywood studios filmed exteriors for *The Truman Show*. It was a peculiar place, always ironic while somehow showing its slip, eventually turning us all into yuppie robots. There was no denying that it was pleasant—the people were friendly and funny, the drinks were good, the beaches were handsome, and there were classy restaurants within minutes. Later we drove down to Cedar Key, Crystal River, Tampa, Fort Myers, Sanibel, Captiva, eventually to the crowded Keys. We got a lot of rain and a fair amount of cold, and it was a nice wintry trip with plenty of car time together, something we'd always liked.

When we got back from Florida, Clare said she needed a break. I guess I was upset by that. We'd had a pleasant holiday, and I was thinking something else. We were in the bedroom at the house in D'Iberville, the TV silently rolling through its news day, story by story.

"It's not a break, exactly," she said. "Just—"

"Fine," I said. "I need to prepare for the new semester, anyway. We have new hot water bottles matriculating at our university. We must attend the flow of hot water bottles into the culture. Lots of apartments to fill up, young fathers to the fathering, mothers for the mothering."

"You have a grave responsibility, Elroy," Clare said.

"Don't be snide," I said.

5

———

I n January we went to a back-to-school party given by some of
the art students. Clare wanted to put in an appearance and
leave, but I drank a lot and started dancing with an Indian girl
who was new in town. She had a red spot on her forehead. The
more I drank, the more I came up with questions about this spot.
I think she did not know what was going on.

Sometime in the middle of things Clare decided that I was
off the reservation again, so she walked out, took my car, left me
at the mercy of my students. I kept after it. Someone took a picture of me dancing stupidly, a Polaroid, and showed it around. I
spent a fair amount of time in the yard. Later, I caught a ride
with Freddie, who took me to her tiny house a half-dozen blocks
off the beach in an older neighborhood—a wood-framed place
up on cement piers, a house with almost no furniture and a bed

arranged diagonally in the bare bedroom. It had that wonderfully austere college-student-lives-here feeling. I managed the usual tour of the bookshelf, tour of the kitchen, tour of the bathroom closet before I passed out.

At first light I woke up in Freddie's bed.

She was there alongside me, her back bare and freckled, her hair shampoo-commercial fresh on the pillow. Her face was turned away. I shoved up a little, propping myself against the head-board, and studied the room. Facing the corner it looked as if the room were whirling around me—no edges were parallel, every-thing vanished into the corner. The space looked abandoned. In the gentle light the scarred walls and bare floors and curiously tilted doorframe were otherworldly. The windows were paired, dust-whitened and covered with vines. The bed sheets were crisp and smelled of jasmine.

For a few minutes I planned my escape, but I must've fallen asleep again, because when I next opened my eyes what I saw was Freddie in a black Chinese robe with red and emerald piping. She greeted me with a cup of coffee.

I sat up, leaning against the pillows, pulled the sheet to my waist and took the cup.

"We meet again," she said. "You went a little crazy last night."

I nodded and sipped the coffee. "That's unusual."

"I know," Freddie said. "I talked to some people."

"What did some people say?"

"Said you used to be dull as a duck, but suddenly you're Mr. Steamy. They don't get it."

"Me neither," I said.

"You were drinking. That's part of it."

"I must have found you very attractive," I said.

She gave me a get-real look. "That's probably not a stretch. I'm twenty-two."

I smiled at her, watched her eyes slit like a woman who knew exactly how attractive she was and could still make jokes about it.

"You were rude to Clare," Freddie said. "Eventually, she walked. Nobody blamed her."

"Did we, uh . . . you know, last night?"

"You wish," she said. "Have a little couth, will you?"

"Sorry," I said. The coffee burned the roof of my mouth. It was bitter and charred. Just the ticket. I rested my head against the headboard and stared at the ceiling where someone had pasted hundreds of light-reflecting plastic stars and planets. Either it had been a child's room once, or . . .

"You stumbled around and said how you wanted to live with me," she said. "You said you were willing to share me, some kind of turn-of-the-century thing, you said."

"Cool," I said. "My apologies. Where're you from again?"

"Taos, Santa Fe, El Paso, Houston," she said. She was sitting on the edge of the bed with her knees up. She barely dented the mattress. "Parts west."

"I didn't used to hang out with students."

"We discussed that already," Freddie said.

"I forgot we're a community here," I said.

"And here we are," Freddie said. "Just the two of us."

"Exactly," I said, nodding. "That's a pretty robe."

"Is, isn't it? My mother's. She had it when she was my age. It's from China."

"Dragons," I said. "I see that."

"No, I mean it's sort of, you know, authentic," Freddie said. "Forties, I think."

"Very handsome," I said. "Suits you. I thought you were an orphan or something—what was that story Winter was telling?"

"I had a mother before I was an orphan," she said, patting the cuffs and straightening the lapels of the shiny robe. "Anyway, it makes me feel like I'm in a movie. That's why I wear it sometimes."

"So you can feel like you're in a movie."

"Right. Old movie. I don't know. You want more coffee?"

I put the cup on the bedside table. "Nope. Just want to sit here and look at you."

She dropped her head, letting her hair screen her face. "You were doing some dancing last night," she said. "After Clare left."

"We are sort of separated, you know? We got old. Sometimes, no matter how hard you try, you can't make things fresh."

"Know what you mean," Freddie said.

"I don't think so," I said.

She made a face. "After a while you quit looking for freshness. It's not important. You don't want to be swept away. Not by a woman, a night, a season, the sea," she said.

"Ah—what is that, some poem?"

42

"No. Sometimes I hang out with older guys." She crossed to the window and finger-opened the blinds. "I hear the same story," she said. "I was hooked up with Mr. Eisenbaum—in English?— last semester, and I got it from him. "

"Uh-huh," I said.

"He loved to explain everything to me, thought he was some kind of walking *World Book Encyclopedia* or something. So he talked and talked and really *instructed* the hell out of me until I just couldn't take it anymore. But he was like you, I mean, troubled with the wife. He couldn't believe my skin, he said. It was so beautiful, he said. He was like nuts about it, on and on. It's like you guys don't really know how to act anymore."

I sat up straight and looked at Freddie's back. "We're just trying to stay in the game. And he's right about the skin."

"Oh, please." She turned around and pointed to the chair on the other side of the bed, smiled at me. "Your clothes. Why don't you jump into them? I'm taking a shower, and then I'll run you home. That O.K.?"

———

Freddie dropped me at Clare's, but Clare was missing. I took a shower, and when I got out she had returned with bags of stuff from the store. I scrubbed a towel around on my wet hair and went out to see her.

She took to the sofa. "Have a good time?" she said.

I sat at the bar with a cup of coffee. There was much greenery in and around the place. It was cool already, the air that filtered into the room had the scent of rain on it. I looked out the back windows and remembered how pretty it was.

"I guess I got out of whack," I said. I touched the coffee to my mouth, just enough to taste it, let it warm my lip. "Nothing happened."

"You didn't make me the coolest bitch in town," Clare said.

"You don't need me for that."

"I don't know," she said, fingering some magazines on the coffee table.

"Sorry," I said. "You get back all right?"

"Apparently," she said.

"I guess I need to get back to my place, huh?"

She smiled not very prettily. "You're a fourteen-year-old, Elroy. Under the rest of this apparatus. That's great."

I shrugged at her, gave her palms up. She got off the sofa, came around to the other side of the bar. I was thinking that I wasn't close to fourteen, and she knew it. I was thinking that when you're our age there are different rules, and that it's too bad, but you can't do anything about it. You give up stuff, forget stuff. You're not in somebody's barn during a rain storm. More and less is at stake, and the game is played with that in mind. The job used to be to cut the distance down to the point where your shirt was touching her shirt, but now it was about balance—distance and balance.

I took my coffee and went to the plate glass that looked out on the deck. "Pretty out here," I said, touching the cup against the window. The touch sounded like a smack, and I pulled the cup away too fast, spilling a teaspoon of coffee over the lip and onto the ruddy wood of the windowsill.

"Need a rag?" she said, turning toward the sink.

"Got it," I said, rubbing the coffee into the wood. "The girl was Freddie. Remember? Winter's friend. In one of my classes this spring. That's a first."

"I hope you enjoyed it," Clare said.

I gave her eyebrows and drawn lips. "I had a good time and nothing happened. I didn't expect you to walk on me."

"Me neither," she said. "I got caught up in the moment."

"It was kind of like the old days, wasn't it? All that high-powered stuff?"

"We don't see it too much," Clare said. "My first husband nearly killed me with it way back when. He was sure I was going around on him. Lost his job because he kept dodging the office to follow me. It was worse after we split up. Kept coming over, spying on me, looking in windows—the whole deal."

"It probably wasn't much fun on his end, either."

"I guess not," she said. She climbed up on the stool I'd vacated. "So, what's next for my second husband?"

6

The second week of spring semester I did conferences with the students on their first projects. I was in my office on the second floor of the old art building, a Greek revival monster built in the fifties, meeting with Edward Works, a smart kid from Maine or Vermont, some place in the East, good-looking, dark hair. I liked Edward because he was rough and quick, and he reminded me of myself. I always like the ones that remind me of myself, even if they're not the best students. But Edward was about the best student I had, so that he reminded me of myself at his age was especially powerful. He looked to me as if he had a chance to make something of himself, and I was always after him to forget school and go to New York. I told him he was going to have to do it sooner or later, and it was better sooner, but he had other ideas. That stubbornness, too, was a shared characteristic.

Edward had transferred in from the program at Florida State. That afternoon we were looking at his new video piece. The late afternoon rain slanted across the campus, across the good, gray sky. I had big windows, and there were trees the size of explosions outside. The rain was splashing these trees around pretty thoroughly. I couldn't quite trace how he'd ended up in Florida, or why he'd transferred to Dry River, but he'd always been kind of friendly, a little quiet. Having students is an odd business; you get close to them, spend a lot of time with them, talk a lot, get personal, spend a few years with them, and then they graduate and get a job somewhere and you never hear much from them after that. It's a little disconcerting because when they're with you, when they're students in the program and you're the professor, they're like friends, but then they just disappear.

"Check this part," Edward said, his eyes glued to my computer screen, a Dell desktop I'd finally pried out of the art school's commodities budget. Onscreen four women stared back at us. They were nude from the waist up.

"Who's this one?" I said, pointing to the girl on one end. "Is that Freddie?"

"No, that's Elaine. Freddie does the next one. You know Freddie?"

"Yes. I know her," I said.

Edward Works wasn't long on the history of art, but he had a lot of touch, an intuitive sense of what might mean something when put out there as art. He was the last guy to be wed to traditions. He photographed interesting stuff in his videos, people doing things, good settings, strange frames, and he set up his pieces in interesting ways in the student shows, made big drawings on photo backdrop paper—whatever came to hand. It had always seemed to me that art was about that one moment, that one quick vision, that sudden realization, and Edward had the knack.

The bed of his audio track was some squashed-together TV news loops, seventies pop music, some techno stuff, punctuated with religious programming—the usual kinds of things a student will do. He had a digital video camera he'd picked up at a pawn shop, and he did the production and the sound on his computer. I could never figure out how he got hooked up with all the girls in his videos—they were always present, always half-dressed. I figured he had a good line of patter. Some of these girls looked kind of young, but I never asked. They just *looked* so young, was my thinking. He called them his bitches, in the fond way, and they loved him for it.

Edward walked like an ape. I envied him his ease with the other students, with everybody, really. He was not just my favorite; he seemed to be everyone's.

"This is pretty interesting," I said.

He laughed, did his Elvis impression. "Why thank you very much," he said.

So we were watching this video with these half-nude women reciting in a monotone some curiously ironic hymn to the disaffected, the *politely* disaffected, something about the tiny whims of the politely disaffected, and listening at the same time to a voice track extolling the virtues of love, relating how love was a wonderful thing, with which I was prepared to agree, when Freddie and Winter arrived together. It was the first time I'd seen Freddie since the party and the sleepover. She'd missed the first two weeks of class. I gave Winter a hug and a forehead kiss.

"So what's up?" Freddie said. "What's with this video?"

"It's Edward's," I said. "You want to see it?"

"We're seeing it already," Winter said, making a what's-with-him? face.

"Yes, ma'am," I said. "Want to sit? Or are you sitting already?"

The two of them dropped cross-legged on the aged plastic sofa I'd commandeered for my office. I took naps on it sometimes. "Turn it up," Winter said.

Edward jimmied up the volume with some mouse clicks.

"I do like your daughter," Freddie said.

"She's only a stepdaughter," I said, shaking my head at Winter.

"In your dreams," Winter said.

"You want to look at this later?" Edward said, clicking on the double-bar pause button onscreen.

"No," I said. "Let it go. We've got an audience now."

———

My idea about teaching was pretty simple: let them do what they want to do, then come along and try to help them make it interesting. I didn't give a lot of instruction, just offered alternatives. The students were going to learn stuff with or without me, and the best I could do for them was candor and encouragement. When I had a painting class I spent the whole time talking about things they could do that they hadn't already done. The best of them read the art magazines and produced the usual replicas of current work, and the worst did portraits in lively colors. Most had little ideas about their paintings. In some cases this did not bother me at all, as when the pieces were interesting enough in themselves. Why should I care how they got that way? Even when the work was weak, or routinely clever, I enjoyed it; I liked seeing what they had in mind, the kinds of things they thought were worth making. It was touching almost all the time. When the work was weak and clever, well, I tried to help them screw it up, in the hope that something else might emerge. They were always responsive, sometimes eager. Students I'd had for a while would tell me in private that I was erratic, making great sense some days, little sense others.

Edward Works had seen a lot of old French movies, Godard and that kind of thing from the 1960s, and had affected a look— disheveled elegance, expensive clothes that had seen better days, good shoes, hair well cut and face cleanly shaved. He was elegant, in a blocky way, and he carried it off with an easy grace.

Having one student like him—crazy about what he was doing, thrilled to be making some kind of art gesture that nobody had made for a few years, a student who could get so in love with a color that he painted everything that color, or so desperate to do something interesting that he'd try anything to get a new-looking picture—that was a prize. It made my classes fresh all the time.

Edward was better than most as a painter and funnier than most as a smart-ass. I would make a joke about Edward, and Edward would make a joke right back. But it was always the kind of respectful joke that a teacher appreciates—he knew his audience. There was, in Edward's jokes, just enough I-know-who-the-teacher-is and I-know-who-the-student-is to make them work, a nicety that a lot of kids in the modern world don't get. Nothing is more tiresome than a pretty good student who doesn't know where the boundaries are.

After I moved, he started coming over sometimes for a drink, or to talk about painting, or to look through magazines and books. It was a kind of familiarity that was new to me, intoxicating because I felt he was as close as I'd had to a protégé.

Where Edward went, the others were sure to follow, so after a time they came, too. Freddie came with him, brought her friend Heidi, and Winter, and then some other friends of Edward's—a handsome kid named Brynn, a shy smart-alecky girl named Cam. So I had a little salon going there for a bit, people slouched around, draped sideways across chairs, sitting on the tile floor with their backs to the couch or the fireplace. Sometimes they would sit around until five in the morning, drinking slowly, deliberately, listening to music, staring at magazines, talking art.

I liked to watch these kids edge toward and away from each other through the night, the small gestures, who was lighting the smokes, who was getting new drinks from the kitchen. It was all very even-handed, but if you watched you could pick up the patterns. They weren't new, they weren't surprising. And through it all everybody circled around Edward. He was the power boy, everyone's favorite. At the school even the faculty adored him, from the potter to the person who taught life drawing, who herself hadn't done a drawing, life or otherwise, in thirty years, to the chairman whose connection to the visual arts nobody ever quite established.

Freddie was a good match for Edward. They all liked her, too, but she was a good bit stranger than he was. Edward Works liked her most of all, but from the looks of it she kept her distance a little bit. The other students envied her jokes and her smile and the offhand way she dealt with practically everything, as if there were nothing to worry about, as if every problem was just too silly to be taken seriously. So she had a fast start. She seemed to get everyone's work in ways that always flattered the artist. And it wasn't phony; she just *understood* better than most. Together, she and Winter were some kind of Martin and Lewis act, some sort of revelation—generous, sweet, funny, always on. Freddie was easy to talk to, knew all the right things to say, laughed readily, took a joke, and delivered a snide remark of her own. In spite of the stories about her checkered upbringing, she acted as if she'd been brought up well, as if she understood her responsibilities and the value of behaving decently when people were treating her decently.

Early in the semester I had a couple of conferences with her. We talked about her painting—she was doing miniatures, tiny six-inch-square pictures with lots of collage and paint work, boxed in polycarbonates. She was interested in midcentury stuff—the Fluxus group, Ray Johnson, Kaprow, Oldenburg when he was doing performances, and in Duchamp and Man Ray and others of that earlier time. In my office Freddie would sit by the window, smoking, holding the cigarette close to the screen in the cranked-open pane so the blue smoke would float away. I liked being with her, talking, sitting in my office through the late afternoons, watching the light in the sky close down. When Freddie was around, I found reasons to hang out with her. I guess it got to be transparent. I was embarrassed. I didn't know where it came from. I told her how lovely I thought she was, just blurted it out one afternoon. I don't know why. I told her she was refreshing and assured her that I didn't talk like that to the other students.

7

When I was settled at the Windswept Condominiums, Mrs. Scree, the neighbor and resident manager, a woman in her middle sixties, appeared at my door with a pie. The pie was very tasty. It was a pleasure to have her around again after all the years since we had lived at the Nile Apartments.

We made it a habit to have dinner together from time to time. I made fun of the way she had run the Nile, the way she was always sneaking around trying to find out what the various renters were up to, what violations of protocol were going on. The apartments were shoddy little two-story, wood-framed things in west Biloxi, but she policed them as if they were fancy, upscale, a Jaguar farm. I was sort of new to the Mississippi coast then, so she and her husband, Carl, chided me for being, well, I don't know what you'd call it—effete maybe.

One night there was some hubbub in the courtyard of the Nile, shouting and screaming and lots of people coming out of their doors to see what was going on. In the open area around the pool, Carl was chasing someone across the brick, out the front gate. Carl apparently lost the guy outside and came back. Three or four of the neighbors who were out to see what was going on had pistols in their back pockets. This surprised me. I remember remarking to Mrs. Scree about this a few days later. She thought it was funny that I was so nervous about all the pistols.

But she was kind to me and fond of Clare, so now, when we had dinner, she always asked about my marriage, about why Clare and I had separated, what the prospects were of our getting back together, why we never had any children, what had happened to Clare's daughter. She rode me or reprimanded me, told me that I'd better think again, because I didn't want to go into old age a single man. I explained to her that I might be content going into old age a single man, but she just shuddered and bopped herself on the head, as if trying to get her brain situated, as if to say no one could believe that, no one could think that.

———

Mrs. Scree was working with an online company, selling a product that was supposed to increase cognitive vitality.

"It's the most important thing in the world," she told me. "Vitality of your brain is the most important. So many older people I know lose that, and then they lose everything. They become like musk oxen. Bumping around through malls, riding around in their big cars, nothing at all in the head. This is something you mustn't forget," she told me.

"I got it," I said.

"Listen, I'm not kidding. I woke up in the middle of the night last night and remembered my MasterCard number without even trying to think about it. It was just right there. That's the kind of thing you want to cultivate."

"You remembered your MasterCard number?" I said.

"Yessir. Digit for digit. Twelve digits. You want to hear it? You want to hear it now?"

"I don't think you ought to tell me your MasterCard number," I said.

"I trust you," she said. "Besides, I don't think you can remember it."

"Thanks, Mrs. Scree."

"Call me Eleanor," she said. "I'm Eleanor to you. We're friends now, neighbors. We help each other. Some day you might need my MasterCard number. You could be somewhere and suddenly be without your MasterCard or have some problem with it. I don't know, it could be anything."

"I think I'll be fine," I said. "I have a couple of cards."

"Everybody thinks they're going to be fine," she said. "That's why I'm talking to you today about brain vitality. I want you to start taking these pills. You don't have to buy them. I'll give you a trial supply. See what you think."

"You want me to take brain vitality pills?"

"Of course. Anybody would. I take them," she said.

"I thought you just sold them," I said.

"Well, I do, but I also take them. They're very good," she said.

"I know. You remembered your MasterCard number."

"Quit it. You're making fun. They're very good for memory, for concentration, focus. For short- and long-term memory. For memorization skills. For visual retention information. These pills just hype up your equipment in a way that can't be done otherwise."

"They hype up your equipment?" I said.

"That's right."

"Is that in the materials they sent you?" I said.

"Yes," she said, somewhat sheepishly.

"Hype up your equipment," I said.

"That's enough," she said.

———

The dinners with Mrs. Scree went from occasional, to biweekly, to weekly—a ritual I was pleased to have. Mrs. Scree knew everyone in the building and knew everyone's business, just as she had at the Nile years before, and that made talking to her quite entertaining.

We had our dinners in her house, on her balcony if the weather permitted. She would ask me about Clare, and she would tell me about the other people who lived at Windswept. I was very glad that she never got messy. So often people will get messy. Eleanor Scree never did. This made me like her all the more.

8

When I was living with Clare, there was always someone around, close at hand, somebody to talk to, somebody to fight with, somebody to go to dinner or to the movies with. There was always someone. There were things to be done. She had plans and ideas I didn't have. Our life was complicated and full of stuff, detailed. We were always busy in one way or another. She was busier than I was, but both of us had things to do, work, things we were interested in.

Now that we were apart, I seemed to have lost many interests. I spent a lot of time sitting at my computer, downloading programs, doing maintenance of one silly kind or another. One night I downloaded several software synthesizers, imagining myself as a musician working on some kind of new music with these programs. I paid $45 for the programs and then installed them and spent the whole night making twenty-minute musical pieces that consisted of allowing these synths to play by themselves. The next night I was out scanning for still other music composition programs. If it wasn't music, it might be photography, boning up on the latest digital cameras, or PDAs, reading reviews of the latest handheld computer offerings from Sony and Palm. And then there were the NFL sites, the literary mags, the Flash sites, the Epinions site, the news sites, the consumer sites, Amazon, the whole range of government sites, the medical sites—an endless array. The Internet had become the collective brain, and I was always poking around in there, looking for something to occupy my time. I got the feeling that if I didn't have a computer my life would be utterly arid. I did not think I would do anything else, read or study or work on some other hobby. A computer is a wonderful and friendly machine, because it's always just a little better than you are. You're always a little bit behind, but it stays right there with you anyway. It allows you to make the mistakes, and then to try to find out what the mistakes are, and then to repair the mistakes. It's always your friend. It quits on you, but it doesn't leave the apartment.

When I was with Clare, I was always surprised at how much activity there was. Perhaps being married is just a better way of being alone. There was a time while we lived together and still did all the things couples do, that she was less interested in me and I was less interested in her. We said the same things to each other over and over—had the same arguments, the same discussions, took the same positions, had the same angles, but Clare seemed more in control of her life, more clear about her opinions, more sensible. In fact, she was sensible to the point of being unpleasant, whereas I was less and less present in the world. I just seemed to wander around. She said things and I nodded. I didn't pay attention. She didn't pay attention to me. We floated through our days in that way.

Like most marriages, ours eventually wore down all the cartilage. We were a hip needing replacement. Bone on bone, grinding, day in and day out. It worked but it was hard.

But after some time away from Clare I wasn't so sure of myself. I sat in my place late at night, looking out the big shining glass doors at the light twinkling over the bay, at the stars in the sky, and I wondered where she was, what she was doing. Whether she was asleep at that moment. Whether she was with somebody. Whether she was talking on the phone or thinking of me. I spent hours like that, just staring out the window. I could only do so much on the computer. I could only look at so many magazines. I knew everything that was in the magazines, everything that I wanted to know, so mostly I just flipped through the pages. I bought them week after week, all kinds, and I flipped through them, looking at the pictures, occasionally reading a caption, once in a while reading a longer piece. I bought so many magazines that throwing them away was a chore. I had to carry them to the garbage chute day after day. Still, I bought, flipped.

Often, at two or three in the morning, if the students weren't there, or coming over, I'd go out on the balcony and think about starting to smoke again. I'd have a drink, and I'd look out at the water, and I'd listen to the cars going by on the beachfront highway, and I'd imagine lighting up a fresh cigarette and taking a deep long drag, pausing for a minute, then slowly letting the smoke wind its way up out of my lungs and spin out into the night air.

———

A dozen years before, after my mother died, my father lived alone in a condo in Tallahassee for about eighteen months. I used to go see him all the time—weekends and holidays. We'd spend time together. Sometimes he'd have projects for us to do. Most times I took Clare, but occasionally I went alone. When I did, I noticed how dry and stingy the place seemed. How his clothes had gotten worn in a way you might expect—buttons off shirts, spots of food dropped on pants, zippers that didn't work.

I remember the mornings best. I would be at the table reading a folded section of newspaper when he'd come down and get his coffee. Then we'd sit there. The morning light poured into his apartment with a vengeance. He insisted on opening the curtains onto the small, concrete patio, first thing, whereas I was the kind of person who was quite content to leave the curtains closed. He'd stand at the window with his hand on his hip, drinking his coffee and looking out at the patio fence not more than ten feet away, on which some bit of jasmine might be growing. I always assumed he was thinking about my mother then, because I remembered one time when I felt particularly bad about a woman I'd lost when I was much younger. Every morning when I woke up, I thought of her. Later, when Clare and I would fight, I worried that this was what I'd feel if Clare and I separated. I knew even then that we would, that the time would come. As it turned out I knew a year before we actually did that we would separate, that we would decide one night to live apart, that I would get a new place, and that I would be alone. And for a year I was terrified about that.

Having seen my father alone all those years before made it much worse. I had asked him questions, once we'd started talking for the day, about what it was like living alone, about what he did and about what he was interested in and about the kinds of things he was planning. He would try to answer but he had no answer, so the elaborate setup, the lighting of his pipe, the deep draw of smoke, the reflection before speech—none of it ever produced a reply. He wasn't planning a thing.

And my father had been, all his life, a man who planned. Planned when he was in his twenties at school to marry my mother. Planned where they were going to live and what kind of work he would do. Planned building his own house. Planned teaching. Planned weekends and outings and holidays for the family. But when I saw him in Tallahassee in that year between my mother's death and his own death, he told me he was planning nothing.

"What're you going to do?" I said. "You've got to do something."

"Why?" he said.

I looked down at my coffee then and tried to think of the answer that could bridge this gap between us, that could break through this rhetorical wall that he'd put up. Why? Why did he have to do something? The trouble then was that I couldn't think of why he had to do something. I knew he was supposed to. I knew that it was psychologically and spiritually and emotionally sensible—reason enough, in my book. But for my father that was no answer. He wanted to know *why*.

Occasionally, in the evenings on my visits, we sat in his living room with the muted TV on, the light shifting constantly, and he'd say, "I've been thinking about going to Mexico. Down to Xochimilco or Taxco. I've been thinking about taking a bus down there and taking some photographs. I remember when I did that before, when your mother was a beast."

I'd watch him then, sitting in his chair, scratching his chin and smoking his pipe, and I'd listen to the crackle of the smoke being drawn into his throat, his lungs. It was odd now that I didn't think of this smoke as violent, I only thought that sitting with him and hearing this sound, surrounded by the aroma of the tobacco, provided a certain kind of warmth for me. A kind of friendly reminder of my father and who he was and what he was about and how he'd been for the last years of his life.

That was such a powerful image for me, that picture of my father, and the scent was so powerful, that I remember thinking once, years later when I smelled some pipe tobacco in a parking lot as I got out of my car, that it was my father visiting me. This was right around the time Clare and I were dividing up the furniture and the pots and pans and the electronics, the sheets and towels—what I was to take to the condo and what she would keep at the house—and I had stopped somewhere to get some candy bars, and I had this feeling that my dead father was there in the parking lot with me, that he'd come back to help me out in the trouble with Clare. So I just started talking to him then. I said, "Hello, Dad. How're you doing? What're you doing here? You coming around to look after me? I could use some looking after. I could use your help."

There in the parking lot I had welcomed my father back into this world.

"I hope you hang around a little bit," I said. "You know I'm kind of doing the *you* thing, going it alone, and it would be good if you'd stick around and give me a pointer or two. You went away pretty quick after Mom died. We didn't get a chance to get things settled, to get a new start. Looks like I'm going to need to do that now."

9

I t was a surprise one windy afternoon in February when I
found myself in the office being fellated by Freddie, who had
stopped by after class. We were locked in my room with the pur-
ple aquascape towel stapled over the glass in the door. Out the
window from my second-floor office you could see only trees, so
we did not bother to draw the blinds. She arrived for a confer-
ence in her tiny jeans and her tiny top and with her pretty hair,
and after ten minutes of talk about her work, about Joseph Cor-
nell, about the difficulty of getting representation, we slid off
topic, and she was kidding me about turning up in her bed after
the party last fall, and I was telling her how much I wished I could
remember it more thoroughly. Shortly thereafter we dropped all
pretenses and had at each other, almost as though we were both

her age. How I managed this, I don't quite know. I do know that bumping around in my office that Tuesday afternoon with Freddie was a heart-stopping affair for me. For her I imagined it was somewhat less dramatic.

Thinking about the English professor she had talked about earlier, I asked her if she hooked up with faculty routinely, and she said, "Not routinely, but it happens."

I nodded as if I understood, as if I appreciated the candor.

What I was thinking, of course, was that this was astonishing and thrilling and I would never get over it and I was guilty of a crime of the worst kind and that after twenty years I had finally gotten to the bottom of my interest in teaching, which all along, under the effort to make my students better, to make them better in their work, to educate them, my fundamental interest in all of the women students, from the very first student to the very last, was to have sex with them, one after another, in seriatim, an endless parade of sexual desire and satisfaction, the play of light and shade on a sexual life I had never had, could only imagine, and which I had wanted, to the exclusion of all else from the beginning of time to the present moment.

I explained all this to Freddie, sure she would catch both the truth and the humor of it, and she smiled and said, "Once a Catholic, always a Catholic."

Freddie was beautiful and sweet and had that lovely hair, a perfectly scarred complexion, beautiful eyes, pretty breasts, exquisite hips, ever so gentle lips.

As I had not cheated on Clare, Freddie was the only woman other than Clare with whom I had had sexual relations in years. To say the sex was stunning understates it. I was terrified when she unbuttoned my trousers, when she unzipped the zipper, when her hand first touched my penis. I was afraid I might not be able to perform, afraid I might go off suddenly like a firecracker with an errant fuse. But that isn't what happened. In moments I was transported to some odd condition of maximum alert. I could not begin to list or report the thoughts that rushed through my head. I know I was fearful. And I was grateful. And I was astonished. All at once. I was overcome with sadness and longing when I looked down at her, touching her hair, brushing it back away from her forehead. My eyes filled with tears, and she looked up at me and saw those tears, and she smiled at me in a way that suggested that she understood them in a reassuring way. But if she understood them, she understood more than I did. As the minutes passed, my thoughts gave way to the sensation, a delirious craziness, a stunning kind of pleasure I hadn't experienced for a long while. Eventually I shunted all my thoughts and allowed myself to accept the pleasure.

When we were done, we lay on the floor between my desk and the windows, wrapped in each others' arms. For a time I thought of nothing at all. No, that isn't true. I was thinking about Italy for some reason. I was "seeing" a shore with rocks, water splashing, old buildings, and old boats in the harbor. Some town in Italy. It wasn't a real town. It was the kind of town you'd see on a television show, *National Geographic* maybe. The kind of town that's the model for an Italian coastal town.

After a while the realization of what had happened came to me, and I became very self-conscious, and I started thinking about the two of us there on the floor of my office. All the dirt and dust. The books stacked, the papers stacked. I was suddenly afraid for her hair, that she might get her hair dirty. Then I kissed her, kissed her forehead, and straightened my clothes. I smiled at her as she straightened hers. Then we sat in that space between my desk and the windows. We laughed quietly. We held hands and laughed.

Finally, Freddie said, "This was one of our better conferences."

"You do very good work," I said. "I think your work's even better than before."

"Thank you," she said. "It's taking on a new edge. I'm pushing the envelope."

"You certainly are," I said.

"I may even be pushing the *edge* of the envelope," she said.

"I never got that either," I said.

She laughed at that, traced her fingers down my forearm. I could have been twenty-two myself. I could have been nineteen the way she made me feel.

"And I say without self-consciousness that you are the most exquisite creature," I said.

"Yada, yada." She did a theatrical wave.

"I know, I know. It's true though. You are kind of breathtaking," I said.

"I like you guys. You're so, I don't know, appreciative."

"Oh, good. Thanks a lot," I said.

"You know what I mean," she said. "I don't mean like there's a lot of you. I just like you in general. I don't mean that I've been sleeping with a lot of older men. I mean, in general older—"

"I know what you mean," I said. "Thank you. Say no more, please. Another word and I claw my eardrums."

"It's not that you're that old," she said.

"I am that old," I said.

"Well, you may be, but you don't act like it. You don't think like you're that old," she said.

"Bravo! He floats!" I said.

"I think we'd better get up," she said. "This part isn't working so well. This part here."

I held her hand and put one of my fingers to my mouth, asking for silence, for quiet. She smiled. We sat that way for a few minutes. I closed my eyes and leaned against the wall. I don't know how long we were like that—it could have been ten, fifteen, twenty minutes. When I opened my eyes again, the room was getting dark. Evening had arrived. She was sleeping softly on the floor, her head propped up on a stack of *Artforum, Frieze,* and *Wallpaper* magazines. I could hear a little wind outside. A tree limb scraped against the glass. I sat there in the closing darkness and smiled. It struck me that this smile wouldn't last that long and I would begin to worry. The worry would drive me crazy for a while. It struck me that I had stepped over some line, some boundary, some edge. I'd stepped out of the spaceship, and I had no idea what was going to happen next. All of these things felt curiously freeing, as if I had done something that would have real consequences that I could not control. This excited me immensely, because it meant I couldn't protect myself as I always had. I couldn't be quite as studied as I was. That things would happen to me instead of me controlling the things that happened. I thought that many of these things might be troubling or difficult or unpleasant. But somehow that didn't bother me. The most exciting was that these were things out of my control, and this was a great virtue for a person gone stale.

I sat there with Freddie for a while longer, listening to her steady breathing, watching her chest rise and fall in the curve of campus streetlight that shined through my office window. I wondered whether this would ever happen again with her or with another student. I thought it probably would, but I wasn't sure. I wondered what Clare would think when I told her. I wondered how I'd feel about it later that night, when I was alone at home, and how Freddie would feel about it. And if I would call her or she would call me or if we'd see each other away from campus. I wondered what it might be like to ride in the car with her, to sit with her on the pier and watch her hair tossed by breezes, to walk hand-in-hand with her around the mall, to eat dinner with her in one of the fancy restaurants in the Beau Rivage. I wondered if I would ever know.

After a time I got up and clicked on the small lamp on my desk, the one I used for reading late at night. Sometimes I liked to come to campus because of the isolation. Because it felt as if there were only the engineers in the belly of the ship at this little school, keeping the engines running through the night. So that evening, there in my office with Freddie, I sat at my desk, picked up a pencil with a metallic blue finish. I scratched the lead of this pencil on a piece of paper at my desk and listened to the noise. I waited for Freddie to wake.

10

After that afternoon with Freddie things changed at the school. They had to, of course. Maybe it was just me being self-conscious, edgy. Maybe it was something about having crossed a boundary and there being no way back. After a time I guessed the students knew that Freddie and I had had this little moment—nothing is ever private in the university—but I didn't *know* it; nobody ever said anything about it. Still, Freddie seemed kind of chilly when she came around, and Edward Works was chillier still. He sort of stopped being the cheerful, flip soul that I'd been so fond of and started keeping to himself. When I'd see them together in class there was some brittle tension, as if we were having a hard time being in the same room together, as if we were magnets pushing each other away.

I had fallen for a lot of my women students over the years, but I didn't tell any of them. I always assumed they knew that I wanted a lot more from them than I asked for or accepted, that I wanted to hold them and touch them and take them to bed and take them out and talk to them, go dancing, go driving, go drinking. I wanted the delicate pleasure of removing their clothes, setting each piece aside, then regarding anew what had been uncovered. Wanted to spend long afternoons with them in quiet rooms with open windows, abrupt breezes, rain dripping off eaves, heaters heating and air conditioners rattling and music and smoke and alcohol.

Freddie was one, but there were dozens of others, and they came in all shapes and sizes—thin as rails, short and tight, bruised-looking, hurt or hard-hipped, curly black hair or straight white. Pretty blond women, striking dark-haired girls, stylish children, homey adults. Women as sexy as magazine models and women sexy in that I'm-not-sexy way. I always resented it when my female students hooked up with guys to make little temporary couples, when they became boyfriend and girlfriend and left me alone, out of the loop, resigned to going home, while they went out and discovered every new and exciting thing about each other, explored every angle, turned each other on end poking and prodding, using all their parts on each other in a maddening rush, then casually smoking and drinking together as they laughed about what they would and wouldn't do, how they moved, how they felt, the scents they liked—this happened over and over in my years of teaching. I couldn't count how many times. So much desire unfulfilled, energy unreleased, feeling unexpressed. How had I managed to spend a whole life this way, not doing what I was desperate to do? I had looked away, played sibling when I was filled with stalker dreams. I had patted shoulders and gently caught hands and smiled, but sometimes, when the light and the weather were right, I had gone to the edge so that between me and the object of my affection there was no doubt what the feeling was. I had always backed away then, slipping into my role as concerned professor, so that now, all these years later, I was filled with memories of women I did not sleep with, women I wanted to touch but had not touched, wanted to kiss but had not kissed, memories of skin I longed to trace with a fingernail, memories of young women who wanted the same thing I did, with whom a caressed cheek had the intensity of orgasm. The women were clear; they were photographs in my memory. That they wanted to fuck me, that they were willing, was almost as good as fucking them. In some ways it was better.

If I'd managed to get over propriety, or fear, I could have had lover after lover from the ranks of my students. I could have lived differently. I might have been a better person, a better teacher, a more interesting artist. Women give you everything. But I wanted something clean, something steady. Maybe my childhood was more frightening than I remembered. Later, the students were less interested. It was easy to tell. I could see in their young eyes, in the way they stood in my office door, in the way they didn't linger after class. I no longer made them nervous. The tension in conferences wasn't the two of us at close quarters, it was her eagerness to get on with her day.

11

A month of discomfort went by, and then one day Mrs. Scree turned up to report that Edward Works had sublet one of the units on our floor, on the back side of the Windswept building, at the far end. Mrs. Scree had understood that the deal was brokered by the Dean of Journalism, who was, as it was said, a friend of Edward's parents.

I expected him to come around any minute, but Edward kept his distance. The salons of the fall had almost completely ceased, and the students had stopped dropping in at all hours of the day and night. That was a little hard to get used to after the last semester, and I got my feelings hurt enough so that I had to make some jokes about it in class, I guess as a roundabout way of getting people to come back. That didn't work. Sometimes I sat there at night hoping some kid would call, or just knock on the door, but after a while that changed, too. I was still hanging out with Freddie, not *seeing* her, but going to dinner, to bars sometimes. And there were a couple of new students in the painting class, so new alliances were formed, and people had other things to do. It was clear that something about the moment of the fall had changed. I didn't think a lot about this—it just was. Edward wasn't rushing to show me his latest video every five minutes. That happens with students—one semester they can't get enough of you, and the next they're looking elsewhere. So Edward didn't come to the apartment, and I didn't see him much at school. He missed classes, but that wasn't unusual. When students were working on their own, they often skipped. I was fine with that as long as they delivered the portfolio at end of term.

About the only time I saw Edward after that was when I saw him out my back window at Windswept, looking down the open vertical space between the two buildings to see him crossing the small courtyard seven floors below. I'd watch him and then hear the screech of the elevator doors and the tired whine of the car as it rose to his floor. Mrs. Scree pointed out some days later that his blinds were never open.

———

One night after Freddie left, I was sitting at my kitchen window having a bowl of cereal. We'd watched the movie *Claire Dolan* on IFC, and afterward Freddie said she had to get home. Rain was headed our way. I heard some shouting down in the courtyard, so I went out the door onto the landing in back, overlooking the open space between the two buildings. Down in the courtyard I could see two people sitting on a bench and smoking cigarettes. After a few minutes I figured out it was Edward and Freddie. They appeared to be arguing. The breeze carried the smoke from the cigarettes away. They hunched over, then sat up, then splayed side by side on the bench, their arms strewn about, their knees propped up. They were in hot conversation. I decided to mind my own business.

A week later I was having dinner at Mrs. Scree's and Edward interrupted. He had come to complain about a woman who was, according to him, filling the hall outside her condo, which was immediately adjacent to his, with boxes, packing materials, crates, and a general run of garbage he thought ought to be taken to the dumpster behind the building.

"So take it out, why don't you?" I said. He was all dressed up, like a French businessman or something. I guessed it was his new idea about haberdashery.

"Gee, thanks, Elroy," he said.

Mrs. Scree invited Edward to join us. "Do you like your new place?" she said.

"It's fine. I'd like it better on the beach side," he said. "And if this woman could play by the rules."

"Gretchen Wills. She just moved in," Mrs. Scree said. "Can we give her a week or two to get settled? I'm sure we can have someone take the things out of the hall."

"She should take care of it," he said. "I moved in and didn't screw everything up. People are always taking advantage of other people, you know? Why is that? It's a simple thing."

"You're right, of course," Mrs. Scree said. "Still, tolerance is a kindness we can afford."

"Some of us," Edward said.

I was taken by his suit. It was impeccable. Usually when you see someone up close, you see, among other things, the flaws in the presentation—the ties don't work, the collars have hairline wrinkles, the belts are off-center, the shoes are scuffed, the sewing on the trouser cuffs may have come undone. There are little stains here and there. Any number of small details give us away, conspiring to suggest just how much of our "self" is manufactured, just how far we are from the person we want to present for public consumption. But on this evening in the world of Edward Works there were no errors; there was not a single hair out of place, no choice was even slightly mistaken, no bit of fluff or dander flawed his suit. His shirt was impeccably pressed and arranged. His trousers were creased to perfection, and his shoes, which looked English, had a lovely warm glow. He looked so good that he was enormously out of place in Mrs. Scree's living room, which was chintz and Naugahyde and small Impressionist prints in gaudy golden frames.

"Where are you off to?" I asked him.

"Dinner," he said. "Freddie and I are having dinner."

"Ah," I said, and turned to Mrs. Scree. "I guess I could help with the boxes. Later, after we eat."

"Whatever you want to do," Edward said, snapping his wrist out so we could all look at a very expensive, very small watch. "I have to go, so I'll leave it with you." He rearranged his cuff and turned for the door.

Mrs. Scree and I stood in the living room a moment before returning to the dining table where our food, looking a little forlorn, remained. As we sat down, Mrs. Scree said, "I think I've lost my appetite."

"No. No, you haven't," I said. "You are ravenous. You will eat until the cows come home. I will help with this corridor problem, and young Edward Works will be happy again."

"He seems disturbed, doesn't he?" she said. "His mother died, I hear."

"I didn't know that. That's too bad."

"He looks good, though. The suit and everything. His nails look good."

"Missed the nails," I said.

"They're pearly," she said. She reached for her fork, beginning to toy with the salad again. "When we finish here, let's take a walk over there and see just how bad the situation is."

"Fine," I said. I was thinking of Edward and Freddie at dinner. I was staring at my salad, where two halves of a boiled egg stared back at me out of their leafy green pasture. I thought them handsome—big yellow eyes, lovely milk-white flesh. Just looking reminded me of the peculiar taste of boiled eggs, a taste I'd savored since childhood. There was special pleasure in the damp dryness of the yolk held in that cooled, almost gelatinous white. I had discussed this with Mrs. Scree on several occasions, and we had agreed that boiled eggs were best served slightly cooler than room temperature. Not cold, precisely, but slightly chilled. So whenever we dined together I could be sure the boiled eggs would have been held in the refrigerator for half an hour or so before serving, in the crisper, where the temperature was carefully controlled. I took up my fork and inserted the tines into the yellow of one of the egg halves, then extracted the yolk whole, holding it at the end of the fork for observation.

Mrs. Scree raised an eyebrow and then smiled, closed her eyes and nodded. "You go ahead," she said. I salted generously and introduced the yolk into my mouth.

———

Gretchen Wills wore a thin halter top and tremendously short shorts. She was in the hall arranging boxes that were lined up along the carpet, stacked four or five high. She had made a mess of things, there was no doubt. She greeted us warmly, shrugging at Mrs. Scree as if to say she knew what a mess it was, as if she were apologizing and complaining about herself, all at the same time.

Mrs. Scree said, "Yikes."

"Mighty handsome work you've done here," I said, extending my hand.

She smiled. "Thank you, sir." She took my hand when I extended it, and her grip was bony.

"We're neighbors now," I said, pointing into her apartment and in the general direction of mine. I was a little nervous. She looked like somebody who had graduated from E!, innocent and randy at the same time. She was all lovely skin, fresh hair, eyes that still sparkled, perfect features.

"Pleased to meet you," she said. "I've been trying to figure out which are your windows, actually. And I've talked with Mrs. Scree about you." She said this with a certain flash in her eyes, a good joke.

"Oh, yes?" I said, turning to Mrs. Scree. "And what has she said?"

"She says you're quiet as a church mouse," Gretchen said, smiling and glancing quickly at Mrs. Scree, as if they shared a slightly different version of this.

"I'm sure I'm flattered," I said.

Mrs. Scree patted my arm. "We've had a visit from Mr. Edward Works," she said to Gretchen. "Your neighbor. He seems to think there is too much, uh—" she paused, looking at the debris in the hall "—*stuff* here. We were wondering if we might help you get it downstairs."

"We could do it together," I said.

"He's a little worm, isn't he?" Gretchen said. "Edward Works."

Mrs. Scree and I both regarded the ceiling at the same time.

"I don't want you to do it," Gretchen said. "I'll take care of it, don't you worry."

"But we want to help," I said.

"Sorry," she said. "I'll take care of it. Don't give it another thought, please. It is a mess. I wish it weren't, but I can take care of it. I'll speak to Mr. Go Down Moses as well."

"I should say in his defense that Edward's mother died just recently," Mrs. Scree said. "I think it hit him harder than he imagined it would."

"That's a terrible thing to have happen," Gretchen said. "I'm sorry to hear that."

"Losing your mother makes you feel untethered," I said.

"How did she die?" Gretchen said.

"Car accident," Mrs. Scree said. "She was driving a car on one of the freeways—I believe she was on her way to meet Edward for lunch—when her car was hit by a truck, one of those huge trucks that carry the great pine logs. She was decapitated. Like Jayne Mansfield."

"Jayne Mansfield was not decapitated, I don't believe," I said.

"Oh, yes," Mrs. Scree said. "I've seen the pictures. People said it was a wig, that her wig was knocked off, but that was just a lie. It was her head."

Gretchen made a face. "Well, he has reason to be upset. It's too bad we have to live with such things."

"Exactly," I said. "I spend a lot of time thinking of things I'd like to correct, things I'd change if I had the opportunity."

Gretchen turned to me expectantly. "Like what?"

"I don't know," I said. "Sorry, I was thinking out loud."

"But what things would you change?" she said. "Really."

"Oh, lots of things. I was thinking of my father, actually. He died years ago, but we were not as close as we had been. He lived in Tallahassee, in a small apartment, alone. I talked to him on the phone often, but I don't think I was as generous as I might have been. He was sick in his last years; I didn't do enough to help out."

"I'm sure you did fine," Mrs. Scree said.

Gretchen patted my elbow. "We all have regrets. I know I do."

"But it would be nice to have a chance to go back and do things over, wouldn't it? Fix the time you wish you'd been somewhere you weren't, or done something you didn't do, a moment that might have significantly changed things. I just never paid sufficient attention. My dad's death was one. If I'd done it better, been there with him, helped out a little, well, his death might have been avoided or been less terrifying for him. He might have had one of those good TV deaths where the person is ready. But he didn't. He was discovered by the plumber who was coming to the house to work on the toilets. Dad had a lot of complaints about toilets, had lots of trouble with them. So the plumber was called, and when he arrived my father was dead, sitting on the bathroom floor facing the toilet. The plumber told me. He was very specific. But I think if I had been there, if I had been with him, if I'd been kinder and tried harder, maybe he wouldn't have died that way."

"Maybe it wasn't as bad as you imagine," Mrs. Scree said. "Think of that."

"Sure," Gretchen said. "Maybe he just stepped over into the next realm right as rain, most natural thing in the world." She stopped and looked at me then and shook her head. "I know," she said. "Doesn't seem likely, does it?"

"He tormented himself about everything. He found trouble wherever he looked. He found things done wrong, people doing things wrong, people not trying hard enough—he found things to complain about. The complaints were always directed at others, but I've always thought he was really complaining about himself, his own regrets. He was easily exasperated."

Mrs. Scree rearranged some of the boxes against the corridor wall. "Many of us are easily exasperated. Edward Works, for example." She rubbed her gray hair, tucked in a tight bun. She loosened it as if to freshen herself.

"There are not many times in your life when you can make a real difference," I said.

"What, somebody turn your dial to Lecture?" Mrs. Scree said.

"Confession," I said.

"Everybody screws up with their parents," Gretchen said. "My mother could have used some companionship, a sweet daughter to take care of her, sit with her. After a while I mostly talked to her on the telephone, so I could get away quick and easy. Shed of her, I didn't have to think about her all the time. That was easier. I called her and listened to her medical problems, but by calling I didn't have to *see* the problems, didn't have to deal with them. We had a woman from Catholic Health Services come in, and we took her to look at nursing homes. Everybody does that."

"I just went along with whatever he wanted," I said. "Encouraged him, whatever he said. I didn't give it that much thought. I figured he wouldn't listen to me anyway."

"Mine always wanted to figure out her future," Gretchen said.

"How old a woman was she then?" Mrs. Scree said.

"Maybe Elroy's age, " Gretchen said, grinning. "Maybe a little younger."

"Years and years," I said.

"You guys are cute together," Mrs. Scree said.

Gretchen looked at her and raised an eyebrow.

"Well, I'm sorry," Mrs. Scree said, slightly flustered. "I must have just had a little fit of cognitive disjunction. Please forgive me. I meant nothing by it. But that's the way it always starts."

"Mine was kind of a tyrant," I said. "My father. Kind of a jovial tyrant, so long as he was tyrannizing freely."

Just then the elevator clinked to a stop down the corridor and the doors hissed open and Edward stepped out and started toward us.

"Speak of the devil," Mrs. Scree said, wagging her eyebrows.

"I think I'll just step back inside here," Gretchen said, backing into the doorway of her apartment.

"Come right back out here," Mrs. Scree said. "I want to introduce you."

"He was kind of a bore, too," I said. "He couldn't help it, but the truth was that's what he'd become. He was plenty ugly in those last months."

"Maybe that's what we all become," Mrs. Scree said. She turned around just in time to catch Edward by the elbow. "How are you?" she said.

"I'm fine, thanks," he said, trying to pull his elbow away from her. He didn't look so fine to me. The clothes were as perfect as before, but he was shuffling along the hallway, too loose, too rubbery.

"I want you to meet Gretchen," Mrs. Scree said. "She's new in the building. Just moving in, as you can see."

Edward gave Mrs. Scree a queer look and then stepped forward and extended his hand to Gretchen, smiling. "Hi. How are you? Glad to meet you. I'm Edward Works. I'm down the corridor here."

"I know. Sorry about the mess. I'll have it policed in a jiffy."

"Forget it," Edward said. "I hadn't noticed. I'll help if you need a hand."

"No. It's fine," Gretchen said.

"We were talking about things we would do differently in our lives if we had the opportunity," I said. "Things we'd like to go back and correct."

"Go back?" Edward said.

"Yes," I said. "Go back in time. How things might have been different if we were at a certain place in a certain time and could do things differently, how we might do that if we had the chance."

"Ah," he said, nodding.

"Time travel," Mrs. Scree said.

"Yes, I see," Edward said.

"I was talking about my father," I said. "As I get older I think more about him, what his life was like after the children were middle-aged, after my mother passed away and he was alone."

"He was probably unhappy," Edward said.

"Just so," I said.

Behind Edward's back Mrs. Scree gave me a shake of the head and a grimace, as if telling me to behave myself. I shrugged at her and smiled. I thought what a lovely woman she was, generous and absent malice.

12

A week later Edward Works stepped over the rail of the interior balcony behind his condo and fell seven floors to his death. It was very late, but Freddie and I were awake; she had decided to stay the night. There was a terrible noise that cannot be described, the sound of a shout and a crushing impact, almost immediately followed by screams, presumably from people who had heard the noise and had gone out on their balconies to see what had happened. Within minutes sirens filled the night air, and people from all over the building came out to stare. Police and EMTs and even fire trucks arrived, and the place was lit up for hours thereafter. Freddie and I had rushed downstairs, not knowing it was Edward, so the discovery, when we got to the courtyard, was very hard to stomach. There is a feeling of disbelief that comes over you, that takes over, and you kind of go through the motions. You do what you're supposed to do, but in fact you're not there at all.

The police wanted to talk to those of us who knew Edward Works, so we sat off to one side with Mrs. Scree, Gretchen Wills, and a few others, waiting our turn. Freddie could not stop crying; I was numb. When the officer called me over, I told him who I was and how I knew Edward, described my job at the school, talked about seeing Edward the week before at Mrs. Scree's and in the corridor outside Gretchen's flat. He had a few more questions, some about Edward's family, and some about other students, and then he took my name and telephone number.

I went back to the holding area, a couple of benches near the elevators, and sat with the others as Freddie, Mrs. Scree, and then Gretchen were interviewed. I think we were all in shock or something like it; you're lightheaded, things are going on around you that you see but cannot account for. Mrs. Scree seemed steadier than the rest of us. She offered that it might have been his mother; Edward Works had seemed, she said, unnaturally attached to his mother and sick about her passing.

"It wasn't his fucking mother," Freddie said, and settled into a steady, quiet sobbing.

I wrapped her up. "Let's go back upstairs," I said.

"That's a good idea," Mrs. Scree said.

I took Freddie back to my place where I made coffee. We sat in the living room for a while, in chilly quiet, the doors to the front deck open enough for the swish of passing cars to cycle through the room. My stomach was in empty knots. I was washed with fear and anxiety, aimless terror, as if Edward's leap was the first of many, as if the whole world might now change into a place more hostile and much less intelligible than anything I had experienced before. All bets were off; we were in another country, one in which everything we knew was suddenly useless. We were on pins and needles, unable to sit still. We'd get up and move from room to room in my flat, check our e-mail, sit in the kitchen, then walk back to the living room, then drift into the bedroom, stretch out on the bed with the light off, staring at the ceiling.

I went down in the elevator a couple of times to keep track of what was happening in the courtyard, but things down there were moving faster than before. The police took a lot of photographs of the scene, and you could see their flashes going off up in Edward's condominium, too, and then the medical examiner's people were whisking away the body, and a crew came in to clean things up. By first light, the courtyard was empty except for a few owners and tenants, stragglers, and it was hard to tell that anything out of the ordinary had happened.

———

In the few days that followed I met Edward Works's father, who was a surprisingly small man with a white goatee. He said he'd heard lots of wonderful things about me from his son. I thanked him and said Edward was a splendid young man, very talented, very sensitive. These things that we said to each other seemed grotesque, not because they were untrue, but because they were so far from being the full truth. I made an effort to say something about how close I'd felt to Edward, how he'd seemed to me the finest kind of person, and that he'd had wonderful prospects as an artist, and that we'd all lost a singular young man, but this whole line of remark seemed way off the point for his father, who'd already had a rich and complicated relationship with Edward, and who, moreover, had recently lost a wife as well. There weren't any nongrotesque things available to us. I introduced Mr. Works to Freddie, and they went through the same kind of ritual, though it had a more personal tone to it, or so it seemed. It was "so, *you're* the girl Edward was so fond of" and like that, certifying that the connection between Freddie and Edward was closer than it ever appeared, something that I had imagined but had never confirmed.

Mr. Works wanted Edward buried in the old-fashioned way, with a polished casket and everything, so he and some people from the school made that arrangement.

The students went through the careful motions of grieving for this fellow traveler they didn't really know all that well. I didn't like watching that. It was as if they were practicing for some real grief they might feel in the future, when their parents died, or their spouses, or just anyone really close to them. They did all the right things, but they were like teenagers smooching for the first time, more charming than true. Their grief lacked something in authenticity. They got too wrapped up in it, too invested, too elaborately grief stricken, and too active in setting up the service and the wake they were too eager to speak at, to remember their dead companion with eulogies and poetry and songs. Their grief and anger and lack of understanding became as important as Edward's death. But even as I privately criticized them, I wondered if that criticism wasn't simply jealousy or possessiveness—he was *my* student, mine to lose. So I went through the motions with them, helped them organize the service at school chapel, and then listened to what they had to say about Edward. Though it sounded right, it was numbing. They wrote their grief with the large brush and said precious little about Edward Works, which made me wonder if I knew anything about him beyond my estimate of his talent, my relatively limited experience of him in the classroom and in the many times he had come up to my place in Windswept. I knew him, but did I *know* him? It was a conventional but nevertheless bothersome question. We'd spoken rarely about personal things. I knew him mostly through our talk about art and artists and works we admired and were touched by. I knew he was a surrogate, not a son but someone perhaps even closer, but I am not sure he knew that. And anyway, that was about me, not him. And there was the outstanding matter of Freddie; there I'd violated an unspoken contract. I could not imagine how important that might have been to him.

At the service, the students were funny and morose and eloquent—pretend adults saying what they imagined appropriate at length and repeatedly. They read poems they had written, homely things, and showed a couple of Edward's videos in which many of them were featured. When it was done, they bore themselves gravely for days at a time. It was just like TV.

Eventually there was an ordinary funeral and a trip to the cemetery and a service there. The odd world of quiet satisfactions, small pleasures, and fresh relationships—everything that I had enjoyed since I had left the house in D'Iberville—started to fade away. Freddie and Winter retreated to the house Freddie was renting, though Winter kept in touch with Clare. Clare kept calling to see how I was, but mostly I avoided the calls, not knowing what I should say to her.

Sitting at my window after the service, I remembered Edward and Freddie in the courtyard, and I wished I had gone down there that night to see what was going on, to see what it was they were arguing about. I wished I had been closer to him then, brought them both back up to my place—I don't know, *interceded* in some way. With students you never know how involved to get in their lives, how much of your attention they can bear. My excuse was that Edward had cooled so much since the first of the year, though I knew that was at least in some part about Freddie.

When Freddie made herself scarce, I just figured she wanted some time by herself, and I was fine with that. I sat on my balcony in the evenings, trying to get back to normal. It wasn't easy. I was rattled and nervous, and the pleasure of being there alone seemed to have vanished altogether. I couldn't feature Edward committing suicide, so I made up other explanations—scenarios in which he hadn't done it at all, but had actually been pushed by a friend, by some other student, by a woman he might have been seeing. It could have been anyone. I thought of many improbable scenarios involving Gretchen Wills, even Mrs. Scree herself. Maybe he had friends I knew nothing about. Maybe they were drinking, there was a party, he accidentally went off the rear balcony. Silly—the police had been all over the place. There had been no party. Just an open door, a step to the railing, a step over.

Sitting on my balcony, watching the clouds ride across the sky, I kept thinking that I might have been able to stop him. Maybe anyone could have stopped him. I imagined knocking on his door as he was getting ready to go out the back, his answering it, upset, or maybe steely cool. We might have had a beer, talked about nothing, and then about what was bothering him—his work, his dead mother, something about me or Freddie—or maybe that wouldn't even have been needed. Just somebody coming by to say hello— maybe that would have been enough to slow him down. Of course, he might have done it later, but he might not have. It was impossible to know what he was doing up in his apartment that night, what he was feeling, what he thought of himself in the world, of his past and of his future, why it seemed to him that going over that railing was the best possible idea. But if someone had slowed him down, just slightly interrupted his course, maybe he could have gotten through that one nightmarish moment; maybe he would never get that close to it again.

I could have been that someone. One tiny joke, one gentle gesture, one little cuff on the back might have been enough to get him through the night, through it for that time and for all the times to come. One of anything might have worked.

———

The next ten days were brittle and uneasy all around, full of abortive spurts of movement, things to do that fizzled, ideas that paled just as quickly as they appeared. I drove by Freddie's a couple of times just to see what was going on there, but her car was always gone. I wondered if she had left town or maybe was holed up in Waveland with that Furlong guy. I drove the coast highway all the way down there but couldn't find his place.

I spent a couple of nights at Clare's, but that was prickly. One night I was there when Winter came over. We had a stiff family meal, and Clare asked Winter if she was going to stay at Freddie's forever.

"I don't know," Winter said. "I'm staying *somewhere*. We're working on some things."

"What's that mean?" Clare said, her tone sharper than she meant it to be.

"Just, you know—whatever. Can't you people just chill?"

I think Clare blamed me for having gotten too close to the students, for hanging out with them, and for somehow connecting them to Winter. "Wouldn't it be better for everybody if you stayed around here for a while?" I said.

"Who's everybody?" Winter said. "And why? Anyway, I'm around, I'm always around. When am I not around?"

So then she was gone and Clare was alone in the house and I was alone in the condo and the world changed around us, without a word, without any announcement or discussion. What had been quiet and restful was now silent and empty. Calling Freddie and never getting her, calling Clare and not having so much to say. I ran the classes, but attendance was off. I asked around school, trying to find Freddie, but nobody had seen her. Clare couldn't find Winter either, though she showed up once at three in the morning to do a bunch of laundry—most of it not hers, Clare told me later.

Then one night there was a long message from Freddie on my machine. "I miss him so much," she said. "Just the way he was always doing stuff, trying things out, shooting pictures of stuff, whatever. You know? I just miss him. What do you think went on with him? How did he get the idea that this was *necessary?* Maybe he just went over the rail and then thought, you know—*Oh, shit!* It had to be like that. I think about him hitting that concrete— Christ." There was a pause, and then she said, "I'm sorry. I should be upset in less graphic terms. We're back in the house now, spending some time. I am. I told Edward about you and me. I can't imagine that had anything . . . well, you know, but it's all I can think of. You don't think that's it, do you? I don't. I don't see how it could be. Anyway, I've got to run. Winter's over in Waveland again, and I need to go get her. Don't worry, she's just visiting. Call me sometime, will you? I miss you. I want to see you. I'm really sort of at loose ends without you. I don't know how that happened, or when—but it did. I guess I could come to class, huh? So—you know. Do something."

13

I went by Freddie's house, but Freddie wasn't there; Winter was there. The house was rattier than I remembered, desolate but well kept. There were new Marks-A-Lot cartoons on the walls—a stick devil, a guy with an X tattooed on his chin, some animals. As before, there was not much furniture, just an aluminum lawn chair or two, a grubby sofa, some beds. A TV with rabbit ears sat on the floor in the corner of the living room. The TV was running when I arrived, but the picture wasn't much good.

"What happened to this place?" I said. "Didn't it used to be a lot neater?"

"Maybe you only saw it under optimum conditions," Winter said.

"What about the cable here?" I said, pointing to the TV. I was thinking of this as a joke, a break-the-ice thing.

"We don't need cable," Winter said. "We can go visit somebody if we need cable. We can get Mom to record it."

So I gave up the clever stuff and tried asking if she was glad to see me.

"Sure," she said. "What'd you think?"

"Don't know," I said. "Clare says you're not coming around much."

"Last week," she said. "Mom's fine. I just need to get a map of my personal space."

"Yeah," I said. "I get that."

"Sure you do," she said. "Why don't you take me for a ride? We can go out for a ride if you want. We'll do the father-daughter thing, or, you know—stepfather thing."

"Good," I said.

"We never did enough of that," she said.

So I took Winter out for a drive. It was late, and I had a feeling it wasn't going to be over soon. We headed past the casinos along the coast highway, then went through Bay St. Louis and Waveland and on down to the west end of the Mississippi coast. There was an abandoned casino site there, where we parked.

We hadn't said much on the drive, but things started easing up. There were six huge steel pilings sticking out of the water, twenty feet in diameter and maybe twenty feet high, just jutting up in space. The casino had been some kind of barge that had floated between these pilings, anchored to them with huge steel arms and iron chains.

We sat in the car, pointed southeast, smoking, drinking coffee from Styrofoam cups. We were on the edge of the water, and there was a rush of wind out there.

"This ought to be a tourist attraction," Winter said. "*The caissons of the casino stand with awesome dignity against the coastal sky*—that deal. We could lease this place and make it into a club for the kids. This is the new, entrepreneurial me, yes? It's a great idea, but it would take investors. Perfect for a stepfather."

"What's with that all of the sudden? Stepfather. You never cared before."

Out at the edge of the water the moon came over the horizon. We sat in the car and watched it lift into the sky, cold, quiet, sifting through clouds. We sat there dressed in our T-shirts and jeans, and we smoked, holding our cigarettes outside the car, and we looked straight out the windshield at the moon.

Winter had her feet propped up on the dash, her T-shirt tight enough so her rib cage was visible when she breathed. "I want to drive," she said. She lifted her head toward the landscape. "This is too much."

"What?"

"Moon," she said, twisting in the seat. "So, what's the deal with you and Mom? You guys still, like, together?"

"Yeah, I guess," I said. "I mean—"

"Not *that* together, huh?"

"Well, I don't know. Sometimes." I said. "Thought you were going to drive? You want to change places?"

"In a minute," she said. "I'm interrogating my stepdad."

"Oh, yeah," I said. "How're you doing?"

She made a face. Moonlight touched the car. She looked out the window, her eyes darting around the darkness. "Why'd you come over to Freddie's, anyway? You come for her?"

"Both of you," I said. "You know, Clare's worried about you, and after Edward, I don't know. Things seem a little shaky, don't they?"

"Well, yeah," she said. "I guess. Guy jumped off a fucking building, you know. What do you expect?"

"I'm never going to be a father to you, am I?" I said.

"More like an uncle or something. You're all right, you did all right."

"Thanks," I said.

"Edward really fucked her up," Winter said. "Freddie. It's not so bad for me because I had all those people die when I was in high school. I'm used to it."

"Who died?" I said.

"Just people I hung out with. Couple of guys, that Terry girl who was the daughter of the gym teacher. Just people I used to party with. But you get used to it after a while. It's not a hard-ass thing, it's just shit happens. I mean, people say this stuff about it, but it passes."

"Edward was way more screwed up than anybody thought."

"Oh, *duh*. But they were friends, him and Freddie, at least until you got into the picture."

"I thought that," I said. "That wasn't so much fun, thinking that."

"I imagine not," Winter said. "Freddie, too. She doesn't talk but she doesn't hide it either. It's O.K. You and Mom are sort of apart now anyway. Freddie's plenty old enough."

"Isn't everybody," I said.

I didn't like Winter two steps ahead of me, but I was proud of her, too. "Freddie's fine," I said.

"Hey," she said. "This is you. This is her. I don't care. I'm not telling anybody anything, if that's what you're thinking."

"Everybody knows," I said.

"Man, you guys are something. Mom knows?"

"Well—not exactly, not yet anyway."

"Ah." She gave her *didn't-think-so* look and then examined her cigarette up close, tapped the ashes out the car window. She looked back at the water.

"Gee, thanks," I said.

"Well?"

I was looking out the window, staring. "We aren't close enough to have this conversation."

"Whose fault is that?" Winter said. "I guess she is kind of young, isn't she? I mean. You know? Would you ever sleep with me?"

I gave her a look. "You don't think I'm answering that, do you?" I shot my cigarette out the window, lit a new one.

"No, really, I'm just asking," she said. "I mean, like, if I wanted to."

"Uh—I don't think so, sweetie."

"What, you're not attracted to me? You always said I was pretty. You don't think I'm pretty anymore?"

"Yes, you're pretty. Still pretty," I said.

"You're always staring at my chest. And at me in my bikini every summer. I see you doing it. Do you think I can't tell?"

"Can we just change the subject here?" I said. "This isn't a good conversation for us to have. You're my daughter, you know—"

"Not exactly," she said. "Really we're not any kind of kin or anything. I mean, it's not that I want to. I was just wondering, if you like Freddie, do you like me, too?"

"Well," I said. "I don't know. I mean, if you weren't family, if things were different—I can't really think of that."

"I've had dreams about you. You know, *dreams.*"

"Sorry to hear that," I said. "Can we go? Let's go."

"So I guess it's a good thing you're not stealing me from my boyfriend, and he's not going out a window."

"I'm not stealing anybody," I said. "I liked Edward, too. You know that. He was my favorite student—well, one of them."

"I hear you," she said.

"Can we just head on? It's bad enough without us getting into this stuff."

Winter got out of the car and came around to my side. "Climb over," she said, opening the door. She held her smoke between her lips as she reached for the keys. "It's hard to figure out what you and Mom are doing all the time anyway. What's with the condo? You guys together or splitting up?"

I was thrilled to be back on safer ground. "It's just a thing we're going through," I said. "I mean, we're apart just to let things, you know, relax a little bit. After you're with somebody a long time, things change. I mean, it's not so important to be with the other person every single minute of every day."

"She wouldn't like this, though, would she?" Winter said. "Freddie."

"It's in the game," I said.

"Freddie know that?"

The car shuddered as she cranked it. In a minute we were back on the two-lane highway that curled around the seawall. The tires crunched as the car speeded up. The top step of the seawall was very close. "You know," she said, "it's not like we're a real father-daughter deal or anything."

"Well, sort of," I said. "Will you get over there? Like, back on the road at least?"

"I mean, the idea that you're, like, you know, whatever or something, with Freddie, well, it's just childish. Things don't work that way. People, you know, get along. I mean, they're friends and everything, but they stay with their own kind."

"They do?"

"Well, there was that Peggy's dad thing, I guess. But he was young and divorced and all that. We only went out a couple times."

"You went out with one of your friends' fathers?"

"Sure. He was hanging with us anyway, and he had some treats, so we just got along some. We went to dinner and to some bars."

"I don't believe this," I said.

"I showed you pictures. Well—showed Mom, anyway. He's a nice guy, owns his own business. And he's not even forty. Well, I mean, he's forty now, but then he was, you know, thirty-nine."

"Peggy who? Which one was Peggy?"

"See, that's the thing—you can't even remember my friends' names. You can't tell one from the other."

"Yes I can. There's the one who wanted to dance topless. And the other one with the tits. And the good-looking one with the really lousy stuff with her father, only she's not so good-looking anymore."

"See, I should never have told you that. About Peggy. I mean, one time she needs some cash so she thinks about dancing, and you're all about that forever after."

"I'm sorry," I said. "I know it's not right."

"I know plenty of stuff about you and Mom," she said. "In the old days. When you guys first got together."

"You were six or something," I said.

"Don't talk to me," Winter said. "I saw some stuff."

I stared out front. The car was back up on the road, but we were going real slowly, and I could hear the tires crunching the sand that had blown up on the road. "So you went out with Peggy's father? Peggy is the thin one with the long hair?"

"Yes," Winter said. "And yes. Platinum. You always ogled her whenever she came over."

"The way you talk that's all I ever did," I said.

"Hey," Winter said.

"So did you, like, *date* him? I don't get this—does your mother know?"

"Sure, she knows. It's nothing. It's just a lot of us were together, and Jack was always around, and he and I got along. We had fun."

"This can't be right. We're not talking about this anymore. We're talking about you and me. I want to sit down with you and go over everything. I've been worried for years, you know? We lived in the same house, and we barely spoke to each other. Every time I tried to say something, I was like some stupid *Just Say No* commercial. I couldn't do any better. I wanted to, but I couldn't. So here, this time, maybe I can, you know?"

Winter slowed the car to a dead stop and dropped her forehead to the steering wheel, then stared out the window toward the Gulf. "It's not like anything happened. We were just playing around, hanging together. You guys have got sex on the brain. You and Mom. You're a pair."

"You sleep with him?" I said.

"Oh, please," she said.

14

I finally got Freddie on the phone, and she invited me over. The days had been going too slowly. I went to school, went home, stopped by Clare's, called Freddie, sat around the condo, had dinner with Mrs. Scree. My classes were quiet meetings during which we just went through the motions, as if after what had happened to Edward we didn't quite know how to get back to normal, didn't know what normal was.

The night was bright with that odd kind of clearness that turns up sometimes in early spring. We were in the kitchen having coffee. Freddie looked worn out, ragged. "I miss him so much, you know? I don't think I knew him very well, but I still miss him. He was like a whole deal all by himself."

"He kept things moving, didn't he?"

"Just kind of vanished—*kazam!* Sometimes I think about him now, and I feel like I'm in there with him, closed in there, under-ground, face up, with all that silk or whatever the hell it is press-ing against me, and I think I want to move my arms or some-thing, I'm trying to get out, trying to get some leverage on the top of that casket—*Jesus.* It's all those scenes from *Six Feet Under* with those guys playing with corpses. I rerun them in my head. Once you start seeing that stuff—"

"I probably should get going," I said.

"Oh, good idea. Good timing. I'm not doing anything, just jabbering here. Forget it."

"What?" I said.

She shook her head. "Sorry," she said. "Why don't you hang around? I've got some videos I've got to sort, some of Edward's, but then we can do something, go out, whatever."

"Sure," I said. "You talked me into it."

"I'm going to start calling you El, maybe. Where did you get this name, anyway?"

"Family," I said. "It happens. It's a tradition. Maybe they didn't know any better, maybe they had a sick sense of humor. Both sides of the family. My father had sisters named Gertrude, Matilda, Alma, and his father was Wardell, and his brother was, like, Don-key Kong or something. Durrell. I mean, that wasn't the end of it. My mother's family was the same. It's like an International World's Dumbest Name contest. I should write it all down for you, the whole history, a terrible car-wreck."

I followed her into the living room and sat down when she pointed to the sofa. There were a couple of new art magazines on the coffee table, so I thumbed through those, looked at this month's work. Like always, it was interesting. People do interesting things. Whenever I looked in the magazines I thought about stuff I'd done and how all art seemed to be the same after a while, how everybody ended up having the same ideas and making the same pieces over and over.

Freddie was leaning over a desk facing her four PCs. I could see her through the doorway in the alcove she called her studio. When I was done with the first magazine, I flicked on the television and then started leafing through the second magazine. I said, "So what're you doing again?"

"Sorting his videos. What about you?"

I dropped the magazine on the table. "I'm watching Perfect Nails. You want to watch?"

"'Perfect Nails' the commercial?" Her computers were in various states of disarray—cases off, extra keyboards propped up, tape drives and backup hard disks ribbon-cabled to the open interiors of the machines, scanners stacked around. "Seen it. Besides, I should do this. You want to help?"

"I don't know," I said. I got the remote, held it at arm's length looking for the channel up and down button. When I found it, I mashed 'Up'. "So, what about staying?" I said, after a minute or two.

"Still here," Freddie said. She stopped her work for a second, turned her head to the side, toward me. "You worried?"

"Always," I said. "But I like visiting you again. How come you haven't returned my calls? Invited me over?"

"I invited you this time."

"I like being out of the house, out of the condo. I like being at *your* house. It's, you know, yours, and I don't have to worry about it."

"So come more often," she said. "You can stay over here sometimes if you want to. That'd be fun."

"What, like—move in?"

"Well, no. That's a bad idea—what am I thinking of? Jesus, Freddie," she said.

"I liked it that time I woke up here," I said.

"Me, too," she said. "That's exactly it. Whatever. You sleep real well, you look good sleeping. Most people don't." She looked at me and shook her head. "Quit looking at me," she said. "I know all about it. I still like it."

"I'd be delighted," I said. "When do I start?"

Through the doorway I watched Freddie watch her computer screens, where jerky images of carnage streamed in different windows. There were some animations, some still shots, hand-colored photos, grainy images repeated and overlapped. She took notes while the speakers played fragments of voices, music, guns firing, sound effects.

She held her cigarette between her fingers, as if it were a weapon. The smoke curled around the screen as she poked a couple of keys aimlessly. She was crying. I went in there.

"You know, you could leave that alone, do this archiving stuff later, whatever. I'm not sure now's a good time."

A new image rolled down one of her screens, a shot of her sticking out her tongue at Edward's camera. In another window some of the World Trade Center video ran, the jumpers.

"Maybe we should *do* something," she said. "Get out of here for a while."

I held out my hand. "Ready when you are."

———

We stopped at a Sonic and got milkshakes. I didn't want one, but Freddie did, and she was driving. We rode along the water for a while, heading toward Gulfport, then cut up Highway 49 and turned right, going out Pass Road. It was plenty cool without the AC. We had the windows down and the breeze rushing through. The sky was clear like HD television—stunning. Specks of light against a uniform dark blue ground. She had Selena on the radio. I liked that, liked that she played whatever she wanted, and I could like it without being responsible for it. We drove around behind Gulfport, heading out for the industrial section, and then made our way to a spot high up on an unfinished highway cutoff. The landscape was flat and black, gridded with city lights between us and the Gulf, black the other direction until the light off of I-10 glowed like a stripe in the sky. There was a steady hiss of crickets out there.

"This is pretty good," I said.

"It was supposed to go straight to Horizon City—heard of that? It's a brave-new-world suburb over on the other side of I-10," Freddie said. "It's like, Hanging Dust, Mississippi. But it's not happening. The road's not going anywhere. Horizon City was over before it ever got started."

"Well, that's kind of typical."

"What is it with this place?" she said. "I mean, is it the I.Q. after all? Nothing ever gets done, does it?" She popped open her door and sighed, "Want to get out?" She went to the edge where the ramp we were on was just cut off, hanging out there connected to nothing with the huge concrete beams jutting out into the air in front of her, settling on columns maybe thirty feet past where the road stopped. And that was it. Thick steel rods stuck out of the ends of the beams. She sat on the concrete with her legs dangling over the edge of the road.

"So, you know, how far is this, like, down to the ground?"

"Don't know," I said. I wanted to touch her hair, play with it, caress it like a high school kid. I always liked the way hair felt. "The bad thing about teaching is that you get attached to the students. And then they just leave. They e-mail you for a while, but eventually they leave and have complete lives in which you don't figure. Like you're some pharmacist they used once."

"Hmm," Freddie said, shaking her head.

"They're always leaving you behind. Makes you feel shitty."

"Poor El," she said, tapping my hand.

"Well, it's true," I said.

"I got it," she said. "I mean it—doesn't sound like fun. I mean, when I remember Father Somebody from grade school, or some high school teacher, what you're saying is exactly right. You're making me feel guilty."

I moved a striped wooden caution barrier, pivoted it on one set of legs and dragged it over in front of the open end of the road.

"What're you doing?" she said.

"Looking out for my fellow man," I said.

She dropped some little chunks of concrete over the edge, hushing me so she could hear them hit. "I just don't know," she finally said, slapping the concrete dust off her hands. "I told Edward everything. I told him we were sort of seeing each other."

"You said that," I said. "Not it. Probably not even nearly it. He had his whole life, he had to decide and he did and I don't get it, but there it is." I looked at the drop at the end of the highway cutoff. Sixty feet down to dirt, machines, stacks of concrete dividers. "You wonder, but you can't know. I saw him the day before, and he was fine, working, talking about new pieces. I made some joke and he made some joke. You know, just Edward."

An emerald sedan with a half dozen kids in it pulled up near us. The driver flicked his lights a couple times and bounced the front end a little. The car was low, neon underneath, giving it that homemade UFO look as it sat there on the freeway ramp.

After a few seconds, the sedan slowly backed away.

Freddie took a minute to look me over, wondering what she could say and get away with. "Why don't you write me a letter or something? A wonderful long letter. I'd like that."

I smiled, nodded, sighed. "A letter. That's a lovely idea. You'd read it?"

"Sure. I'd like a letter from you. You're something special, you know? Patience—and you're always solidly there. That's something rare."

I skidded a rock off the edge of the highway. "Missed my calling," I said. "I could've been a parish priest. I would have liked that. You're safe, so you get to help other people all the time; that's a lovely idea for a life."

"I spend a lot of time thinking about you," she said. "Too much time."

"That's nice to hear," I said.

She struck some rocks against each other as if trying to start a fire the Boy Scout way. "You knew though, right?"

"No, not really. I just go along, whatever's there. You've been very sweet to me, but, you know—"

"What?" she said.

"I don't know," I said. "I don't know what I even was going to say." Somewhere not too far off a jet engine shrieked as a passenger airplane prepared for landing. I looked out into the darkness for the airplane's lights.

"I miss the Mass," I said. "Miss being ten or twelve in my parents' house, everything in order, school, church. All that stuff. It's like that was another world. As I got older, things changed and it started to be my turn and I didn't like it anymore."

"Your turn's over, isn't it?"

"Thanks, dear," I said.

"I was kidding," she said. "You're a young rascal, aren't you? You're ready for Freddie." She was lovely in relief by car lights against the night sky.

"I don't know," I said. "I might like to be. But I may turn out to be a confessional and Latin mass guy. I remember the padded rubber stuff on the kneelers. I am the last true Catholic."

"No way. I was a Catholic way later. My first real boyfriend was Catholic, so we were like these fifties kids zoomed ahead in time. We were deadly serious. We prayed like crazy, hard as we could. We used to hold hands and say the Hail Mary together, like in a swing on the porch. Of course we were fucking, too, but we put everything into that Hail Mary."

"Amen," I said.

"Here's what I think about love," Freddie said. "It's fine, it's great. But it always has egg on its face."

"Huh?" I said, holding my hands apart, asking for the translation.

"You know, it never works, and it's always sort of dry and desert-like, full of unhappiness, bleeding edges, the sense that it would be great if you could just feel it full out, but you never can."

"Oh. Right," I said. The low rider was back, creeping up the incline toward us. I said, "Figure we'd better get out of here?"

"Yeah. We're having turf issues." Freddie did some handwriting in the air with her cigarette. The ash glowed as she swung it.

"What's that?"

"Telling them to fuck off," she said. "Writing them a short letter." She got up, flipped the cigarette over the edge, took my elbow as if to lead me back to the car. "Let's go, O.K.? Before I explain everything. I get carried away sometimes. Don't get me carried away. Religion will do it."

We headed for the car. I started to put an arm around her, then thought better.

15

Freddie and I started hanging out together at school, having endless conferences, or just private afternoons in my office, lounging around. We were a little too conspicuous, but it was the art department, after all. When we weren't there, we went to eat or went to the movies, or we drove around looking at property, pulling those "Take One" sheets out of the real estate brokers' boxes, or we went to the casinos. I was at her house all the time, though I didn't take her up too often on her offer to stay there. I don't know why. I was over there, but I always left when it seemed that she was starting to fade out, or I'd stay until she fell asleep and then slip away. I couldn't figure out what I'd do if I stayed there all night. When Winter was there, it was too awkward to stay. Sometimes Winter tried to sit around and chat, but more often she went to bed early, or at least disappeared into her room, just as happy to be free of me. I guess I was pleased to have somewhere to go, to be able to head back to Windswept where I had a lot of things to do in my highly ordered second life. The pleasure had sort of come back there. I was comfortable again, though I was spending a fair amount of time thinking about Clare, and our marriage, and remembering how things were when we first got together, and thinking about the other time we almost separated.

It was when I was just getting tired of being the artist, tired of making pictures all the time, storing them in a closet. I had cooled off on everything, really, so I was just teaching at Dry River. The salary in those days wasn't all that good. I was unhappy about things at the school—who they hired, who they let go. I was maybe too involved with the art department. You get that way if there's nothing else going on. You suddenly decide you ought to fix everything, and I was not graceful or charming, and every idea I had was really an accusation. I don't know what was going on, why I cared so much, but I did. I made myself miserable, and Clare was tired of hearing about every single thing I was going through. Whatever was pissing me off about the school was the last thing Clare wanted to know. We'd been together four or five years by then, I suppose, and maybe our life had been an array of small disappointments for her. You live with somebody and you never really know. I mean, you can't expect them to come right out and tell you what they think, because there's always the chance that they're looking elsewhere, looking at alternatives, and they don't want to tell you and you don't want to hear, because if it were out in the open it would change everything. So you keep quiet, and she keeps quiet, and you play through.

We got married because of Winter, the child of a previous marriage. I loved that phrase because it released me from the burden of parenthood. I guess that's not so pretty, but there it is. I think Clare and I liked each other and figured the world was a place we could navigate together. But it wasn't that easy. The marriage did not make the world simpler. We were just like we had been before we got married; I don't know what gave us the idea that we would be different.

When Clare's mother died we had to drive out to Utah for the funeral. I canceled my classes. Winter did not travel with us. We were there for four days, and after we left I could barely remember what her father looked like. I remember that everybody in the town wore khakis. We camped out in the car on the way out and on the way back. That was fun. We slept in the car. We pulled over at highway rest stops. We had a new car then; I can't remember why. The seats were comfortable and went all the way back, so we could stretch out. That was the best part of the trip.

———

In those days, when we were fighting, Clare would call at school and say, "I want a divorce. I don't want you to come home tonight or any other night. I don't want to ever have to see you again. I don't want to hear your voice. I don't want to smell you. That's it. It's over." Then she'd hang up, leave me there on the line.

I hardly knew what to do. You're having your own troubles, and suddenly your wife is calling to playfully ask for a divorce. Sometimes I'd call her back.

"What? What's that?" I would say. "Are you being whimsical? Have you been drinking?"

"Oh, yeah," she'd say. "I do that. I drink the Jack Daniel's until I am blotto. Makes me feel things, gives me ideas about the world. Helps me to see the world in a new way."

"O.K. Sorry. That was stupid."

"Ding," she'd say.

"So why did you call?"

"I wanted to express my feelings," she'd say.

"So you don't, like, really want a divorce?"

"I don't know. What about you?"

"I'm fine," I'd say. "Good to go."

And then there would be some explanation—her mother, or trouble with Winter, or she was lonely—anything, as long as it was something simple. We'd talk for a while. I'd have my feet on my desk in my office at school, and I'd be pushing art books around with my feet, rearranging them. And we'd spend some time together, and that would be it. Problem vanished.

Early on, after we left Mrs. Scree's apartments, we had a bungalow on the corner of Decatur and 10th in Biloxi. It was gray and was built in the forties, redone in the seventies. It seemed nice to me, homey. Sometimes in the fall or spring we left the windows open and turned on the attic fan to draw breezes through the house, breezes that reminded me of nights at the beach when I was a kid. We lay on the bed together with these fast winds blowing over us. The smell of the place was kind of old— old wood, old flooring, old fixtures—and the age and the salt air reminded me of when I spent weeks at my grandmother's.

When I stayed with my grandparents in Florida, my bed was on the sleeping porch. I played with my grandfather's shotguns. My grandmother was just some stranger to me, almost like a neighbor or something, some woman my parents knew. She waddled and she talked about people I didn't know. Grandmothers do that. She smelled sour and talc-y. She was wrinkled. She was squat, bossy. I could never feature her with my grandfather, who was a lanky, easygoing sort. A handsome guy, a ballplayer, triple A. Not the kind of guy you'd see with a woman like her, ordinarily. But she might not have been wrinkled all her life. I guess that's a possibility. They had a black woman who cooked for them— I don't remember her name. It was one of those Southern member-of-the-family deals. They liked this woman and the woman liked them. My father ran the car into her by accident one time. That caused some trouble.

In those days in Florida there was more light than I have ever seen in any other place. Outside, everything was baked-white light and bristling reflections. Sand everywhere, bright awnings, green shutters, tricky breezes. Inside, everything was dark and heavy—wood and brocade and thick rugs. It wasn't bad. Thinking back, I wouldn't mind being there. I wouldn't mind taking

Clare and moving back there and running a restaurant, maybe an oyster joint someplace up off the beach.

———

So that time a few years after we were married was the only other time we ever really got close to separating. You never think you're going to dislike someone you've been living with for that long. You know stuff about them, spend so much time with them trying to make things O.K. The idea that you'll end up not liking them is strange, remote, like some ship you don't expect to come into your waters. Somebody you don't expect to see in the neighborhood. But that's what happened with Clare and me. We went to bed at night and couldn't quite remember why we were together—what she saw in me, what I saw in her. I didn't hate her, but maybe it was worse—not caring about her, cutting her out of my life. She might as well have been some woman in a Jeep Cherokee somewhere. We were just so tired of each other.

Back then I made everything into a romance—almost everything. I shied away from the students, but every girl I saw in every parking lot was just about perfect; they all had great hair, lovely eyes, long legs. They all walked in a way that was inviting, and their skin was uniformly perfect or, better than that, roughed up in an exciting way. I couldn't get enough of women with bad skin, long subsided acne, barely concealed scars—especially if the rest of the get up was kind of perfect. I saw every woman as a replacement for Clare, a new start, a rescue from a life that was—to be kind— dull. An invitation to a life without the difficult stepdaughter.

Once I wrote my telephone number on a credit card receipt for a particularly attractive waitress at a Mexican restaurant. She was a student, it turned out, at another school. We had a date. I took her out to dinner, and she was dumb as a truck. She lived in a tiny apartment in a field of apartments with two friends who were also dumb as trucks, so it was like a parking lot in there. But she was pretty. Her skin was lovely and her hair fell beautifully around her face, her cheekbones were high, clear, defined, she had a few freckles across her nose, and her lips said she meant business. She had good, strong legs, thin, cut, and she walked like an athlete, with that confidence, that nonchalance. It was a very dissonant night. I'd get carried away by the way her arms moved, the way her backside moved, but then I'd get brought back to earth in a conversation about her history exam.

Sitting in the restaurant with her for two hours was sort of difficult. When we were done, I took her by the house to meet Clare—God knows what that was about, what I was thinking. Clare had okayed the "date," naturally. I suppose she knew what was going to happen. When we walked into our house and I introduced the girl, Clare was very friendly, offered coffee or a drink, and the girl asked for a beer. We sat for a few minutes in the living room, and then the girl excused herself and went into the guest bath. A few minutes later she poked her head around the door and signaled for Clare. We looked at each other and shrugged, and then Clare got up.

It turned out the girl had started her period and didn't have anything with her. She'd messed up her white pants, too, so Clare had to lend her some sweats. That was hard to get over, and shortly after that I took the girl home, kissed her goodnight at the door, left feeling relief.

Clare looked pretty good after that. If she'd been new to me and I'd seen her for the first time, I might have followed her around, left her my number. But that part was already over for us, though the idea that things were "over" was sort of new to me. Before Clare, I'd changed girlfriends a lot, so getting to a point of breaking up wasn't new, but staying after that point was. I wondered if it was the same for her, and for others.

————

As it turned out, that trip to Utah somehow settled things down between us. Driving the empty streets of small towns through the night, going out there, it was like we were riding through toy streets and plastic towns in a life-size version of the model train sets I'd had as a kid. The green of the grass was bright plastic green, the white of the bricks was viciously white, and the roofs were all stop-sign red. The street lights in these towns seemed wasted over empty streets in the middle of the night, going red, going green, going red. Silly business, but beautiful in its way. It was as if we owned the whole country, town after town, as if there wasn't anybody else around; it was ours. Little cats ran across the street in the middle of the night, hopping almost, their back legs trying to get ahead of their fronts. Sometimes we stopped to look at them—orange or black or gray tabbies. And the early birds were out in these towns—guys in milk trucks, pickups, people just coming home or making runs to the dough- nut shop. The sky was a perfect black with millions of tiny dots all the same size. It's something, the sky at night. On the high- way, only headlights lit the way. We were enveloped by the soft darkness. The rare motel on the roadside was supposed to make you feel something, and that started working for us on the way back from Utah. We liked it out there, liked it together. We started to get comfortable again, and we saw a world and thought it was pretty and ours, and we knew that we belonged together, and that had held us for a good long time.

16

One night when I was over at Freddie's, Noble Furlong arrived in the storied Cadillac convertible with a wiry guy named Victor, who was mid-twenties and small, with too much hair done up in the previously modern *I've been sleeping* style. Victor was a pal of Furlong's and a regular at his club, and he seemed to have his eye on Winter. She knew him a little, apparently. He was planning a bus trip to Memphis, and he was trying to get her to go with. When that didn't work, he just needed to ride to the bus station.

"How come our friend can't take you?" Winter asked.

"He is Mr. Noble Furlong," Victor said. "And he does not speak bus station."

"Good work if you can get it," I said.

So Winter and I took Freddie's VW and headed out onto Beach Road with R&B music pouring out of the CD player, Victor lodged in back. Victor was wearing road clothes, a backpack, big shoes. He'd originally come by the house to get a sleeping bag, a blue one, that he'd left on a previous occasion.

Winter was explaining things to him. "See, I used to go around and introduce myself as Rocky and Bullwinkle. This was a thing I did."

"Uh-huh," Victor said.

"I was Rocky *and* I was Bullwinkle."

"Uh-huh."

"You ever see the show?

"Never did," he said. "Heard of it, though. And *Rocky* the movie, and Roky Erickson . . . "

Winter blew a wad of gum out the window at a billboard, using her fist like a blowgun. "Right. Cool—knows the Elevators. Put that in the report. So what's with the Elvis trip, anyway?" she said.

Victor wagged his fingers over the back of the seat at the road ahead. We were driving past a huge SAY GOODBYE TO LONELINESS sign. The streetlights glistened. "Home," he said. "So how come you guys don't drive me up?"

"Work," I said.

"Plus," Winter said, "we got to take care of stuff. Some videos. A friend of ours was a video artist."

"I used to do computers," he said. "Software manuals, that kind of thing. For games."

"*Doom?*"

"No. *Doom* sucks. But we did others. They sent us the shit, and we played it for a while, then wrote the manual. Nobody ever looks at manuals, so we got away with murder."

Winter tried to give Victor a high-five. "Whoa. Cool. What a deal. I'll bet I could write the hell out of those manuals."

"Yeah. You probably could."

That was about it. As we pulled into the parking lot outside the bus station, Winter poked a finger into my knee. "I need to talk to you, buddy," she said.

"It's a good thing I came, then, huh?"

"You betchum," she said.

The vacuum wheeze of air brakes was loud at the bus station. It was near midnight. Victor stood on the curb and watched us pull away. Winter fingered a sheet of note paper.

"What's that about?" I said.

She unrolled the paper. "Phone number," she said. "Never can tell when you'll need a pal."

"He had a hungry look," I said.

"Nah," she said. "Well—maybe."

We drove a little while because Winter had to make a couple of stops, and I wanted to pick up a change of clothes at my place. She filled me in on Furlong and what he was doing, which was trying to get her to come back and tend to his domestic needs. She was giving him the brush-off.

"It's Freddie," she said. "She's a little sideways about you. And I don't know what your deal is."

"Yeah. Me neither," I said. "What's it look like to you?"

"You don't really want to know," she said. "Looks like all the rest of the shit that happens."

"I like her," I said.

"That's a start."

"No, I mean—really. She's good. What does she think is going on?"

"Nah," Winter said. "You're not going to get me that easy."

"Jesus, Winter," I said.

"We've all been there," she said.

"That's not fair," I said. "I mean, I've known her a while; we go around and do stuff. She asked me to stay at the house."

"That's what I know," Winter said. "That's why I'm asking."

"So what's the problem?" I said.

"I'm not threatening you," Winter said. "I'm just laying it out for you. Just plain."

"I appreciate that."

"We've been through some hard shit, you know. We're tired of hard shit. We want some easy shit for a while."

"I get that," I said, thinking it was strange and satisfying to have her talk to me this way.

"I hope so," she said.

———

When we got back to the house, Freddie was sitting in a metal chair on the front porch in a cone of yellow bug light. The house was painted several Gap catalog colors—taupe, maize, clam—

and at night they seemed super-subtle. Sand surfers walked by carrying their surfboards, headed down the road to the beach.

"Hey, look at you, you're back," Freddie said. "I wasn't sure." She pointed at a potted cactus. "What happened to our key in the pot here?"

"Victor got it," Winter said.

Freddie grabbed my hand. "Clare called and said to tell you hello. Said to tell you whatever you want to do is O.K. with her. She's with you all the way. She was looking for you, Winter. I get the feeling she's tired of us young people."

"I'll call her," Winter said.

Three brown ducks waddled through the sandy front yard, squawking. We waited for them to pass, then went inside.

The phone rang. Winter signaled me to get it. I did, while she went into the next room, but it was for her. "For you," I called. "It's your new friend Victor."

She was back in flash. "Hey! We just dropped him at the bus station."

"Tell me," I said.

Back in the hallway there was a dial telephone in a cubbyhole in the wall. Somebody cared enough to find this phone. There was a small Virgin Mary statue, blue and white, in the cubbyhole with the phone. Winter took the receiver and noodled on the wall with a Marks-A-Lot she'd picked up from alongside the phone book. She drew bloody pirate swords. "I guess you can't get your minds off me," she said into the mouthpiece, giggling. "You think about me day and night. What's it been, thirty minutes?"

I watched her on the phone. She was a natural. Freddie stepped through the doorway into the hall, then slid away—in and out, repeatedly. She signaled me. "I need to talk to you. I need your help."

Winter waved to us to shut up or get out of the hall. "No, I thought, you know—Elvis," she said into the phone. "The pilgrimage." She touched up a drawing of an anorexic dog she'd done on the sheetrock.

"Fuck him," she said a minute later. "He's dead. Fat and dead. You—you're one hundred percent alive." She shooed us, but we didn't budge. "So, why not stay a day and see what happens? Something could happen." She eyed us, scratched at the wall, listened. "I don't know. *Something.*"

———

The three of us went into the kitchen where there was another statue, this one a Wal-Mart concrete Jesus, two feet tall, its face scribbled over with black marker, the eyes painted crazy red. The kitchen was spotless but worn. "So," Freddie said, waving an introductory hand at me. "Elroy's here."

"Big as life," Winter said. She looked at me kind of exasperated-looking. "Victor's staying at the bus station."

"Elroy's loved me all his days," Freddie said.

"Nah," Winter said, looking in the refrigerator for something to eat. She pulled out a carton of eggs. "He's messing with you."

"I want to call Clare," I said.

"You saw the phone," Winter said.

"It is permitted," Freddie said. She pointed to the eggs Winter was cracking into a bowl. "Put some milk in those."

"No way," Winter said.

I headed back into the hallway and dialed. I petted the Virgin Mary while I waited for Clare to answer. I scanned the wall around the phone, checking out the drawings.

When she answered it was such a relief to hear her voice that I was startled. It was a freak of timing, I guess, one of those things where everything is in perfect alignment; people only say the right things, nothing but pleasure and comfort. I told her about talking to Winter, and she said she'd heard. She asked how I liked my new freewheelin' self, which was an old joke between us, making fun of a hundred different things. That just stopped me in my tracks. I said, "I'm doing okay, but these kids today, you know, they live hard. They write on walls."

"Ah, baloney," she said. "We wrote on walls back in the day. We spray painted 'em. What, did you forget?"

We talked a little. I told her about the house, the statuary, the dusty aspect of things. I told her Freddie and I had been out on an unfinished freeway.

"Now there's an old trick," she said.

"Yep. So this car came up, one with neon underneath."

"You'll never get over that, will you?"

"It's such a charming thing," I said. "Such a funny idea."

"You always wanted one of those, Elroy. Maybe I'll get you fixed up for your birthday. You like lime or lavender?"

"Ask again later," I said.

Clare wanted to know if I was holding up O.K. about Edward Works, and I said I was good enough.

"It's awful, but it's no reason to nosedive completely."

"I'm thinking it was murder," I said. "I'm trying to get the police interested in that."

"Good idea," she said. "Maybe he was secretly seeing Styrene, Mistress of Danger. You can never tell about women. They lead men to ruin, that's their stock in trade. I don't have to tell you."

"Have you been watching too much TV?" I said.

"I shouldn't joke," Clare said. "But I wasn't joking about him, O.K.? You get that?"

"Yes," I said.

"This world is a dangerous place, Elroy," she said. "So I am glad that you are out there in it and I'm at home here with Wavy, who offers his regards, by the way. Today on our walk he acquired a turtle shell, abandoned. Very stinky, it was. I had to trick him with ice cream to get him to drop it."

"Wavy has a mind of his own," I said.

"A pebble," she said. "But utterly his."

We went on a few more minutes because I just wanted to be with her, somebody more or less at ease in her skin. Like always, Clare kind of staggered me with equanimity, a much unheralded virtue in my book. She had something interesting to say about the plumber, who had visited earlier in the day, and some kind words for a neighbor who was selling her house. I stayed on as long as I could, but after a while she had to go, so we said goodnight.

I placed the receiver in its cradle. No one was around. I'd promised Freddie that I would stay the night, so I went to the guest room and took things out of my overnight bag, hung a shirt neatly in the empty closet, went about the business of making myself at home.

Minutes later Freddie was in the doorway of the room, looking at me stretched out on the mattress. "Set your stuff up, did you?"

"I put everything away. I know how you like a straight house."

"That's you, Elroy. I'm pigsty girl." She checked the closet and then went into the bathroom.

"I have no problem with that," I said.

She came out of the bath unfolding a perfectly folded towel.

"I moved those around," I said. "I figured I'd use the blue and you could have the white. The blue goes better with the paper in the bath there."

"I knew that," she said. "But it gets depressing, things always going together." She motioned toward her room. "You coming in there or you staying in here?" She refolded the towel and dropped it on the end of the bed.

"Here, I guess."

She smiled, ran her fingers through my hair and left without looking back. I was glad to have the room to myself. I stayed right where I was on the mattress and tried to figure out what was next, what might happen, what I was supposed to do. I looked around at the dusty beat-up room and missed my perfectly clean flat. I liked thinking about it, the fresh paint, the arranged furniture, and the neat stacks of things. I was eager to make new stacks—magazines, books, postcards, boxes of things. What a pleasure that would be.

———

We went for breakfast at the IHOP that was downtown near the bus station. It was late, sometime after noon. The place was filled with weird-looking people—guys with chains all over them, kids with nose rings, brow rings, cheek piercings, gauged ears, tattoos out the bum, and those big pants that hung around the bottoms of their asses. I hadn't been to IHOP for a while, so it was startling to see that this was where all these kids ended up after their moment. A gum-smacking waitress was zinging around. Our table had a boomerang-pattern top and red vinyl seats. We ordered sodas and platters of fries.

"O.K., here's the deal," Winter said. "I'm asking Victor if he wants to stay. He can bunk on the couch. That's my decision."

"Go, girl," Freddie said.

"What? I'm not doing anything. Just gonna hole up with him for a few days." Winter swung her backpack around and slammed it on the table. She dug a jar out and smeared on skin cleanser. She was all Spandex and Converse and shirttails.

"What's this about?" I said.

"Full disclosure," Winter said.

"It's about Winter's harvest," Freddie said.

"You are such a prom queen," Winter said.

Just about then Victor showed up outside the diner, peering in the window. He saw us and waved.

"He's a nice guy," Winter said. "C'mon. It'll be fun."

The waitress showed up. "How're we doing, kids?"

"You mean with the food? This onion ring loaf is so great," Freddie said.

"Uh-huh. I hear that," the waitress said, walking off with her pad held high.

The girls rolled their eyes in unison.

When Victor got to the table, Winter said, "So, Victor. What's happening? What's shakin'? What's doin'? What's the deal? What're you up to? 'Sup? Howzit?" She jutted a hand out to shake.

Victor took it and smiled distractedly. "What're you guys eating?" he said.

"Whatever you want, I guess," Winter said.

Pretty soon the table was full of pancakes, hash browns, bacon, eggs, coffee. Outside the light softened through thick gray clouds.

"I didn't get much sleep," Victor said.

"So what are you going to Memphis *for,* Victor?" Freddie said. "I mean, if you ever go. The usual?"

"I thought you were *from* Memphis?" Winter said. "Besides, the King was way too dead before you were even born."

"Was not," Victor said. "I was, like, five."

He made as if to do a little bit of Elvis impersonation, but Freddie said, "Man, that thing is huge," the Tiny El joke that

Edward always used to do, and that sucked the wind right out of Victor's sails.

He waved a fork with three dripping squares of pancake on it. "I gotta go," he said. "I've waited long enough."

"You don't have to," Winter said.

We pushed food around a while longer. After that we settled up the bill and bumped out to the parking lot where Winter and Victor moved off in the direction of the bus station.

Freddie and I sat in the car. "Too much monkey business," she said. "This is not in the game."

"What?"

"This," she said, motioning out the windshield toward Winter and Victor. "Don't you, like, worry about her?"

"She does fine," I said. "I've got a new respect for her, you know? She knows what's what. Besides, he's leaving."

"Maybe," she said.

It took them a while, but eventually Winter and Victor separated, Winter got back in the car, and we took off for the house. Winter went to her room right away and left Freddie and me alone. We watched a cartoon running soundlessly on the television for a few minutes, and then Freddie bopped my head and said she was washing her hair.

"You want to watch?" she said.

"Don't know," I said. "I could. I could watch. But I don't have to if you'd rather, you know, do it by yourself. I don't know, what do you think?"

She made her fingers like a picture frame, looked at me through it. "What I see is you," she said. "Holding the bag." Then she left the room.

I stayed there with the cartoon TV for a while, then went to the guest room where I'd slept the night before and stretched out on the bed. It was nice just to let everything melt away. When I woke up it was late afternoon. I went to the bath and splashed water on my face, then looked for Freddie.

She was in the living room. I sat down next to her and asked what she was doing. "I took a nap and washed my hair," she said, pointing at her hair, which was still wet.

"I remember now," I said.

"You were sound asleep. I checked."

I sort of touched the hair.

"Quit that," she said.

Winter reappeared, looking fresh-scrubbed, but the clothes were the same. Patchwork. Her hair was spiky, black, Asian-looking. Another new look for her. When she moved over by us and batted at my arm, I tried to play with *her* hair.

"Quit screwing around," she said. "We need to call Furlong," she said to Freddie.

"Why?" Freddie said, without looking up.

I got up and headed for the kitchen. "Anybody want anything?" I said.

"I could use a beer, sir. If you don't mind," Freddie said.

I gave her a look.

Winter put her head on Freddie's shoulder. "Is Elroy O.K., do you think?" Winter said.

Freddie reached to gently caress Winter's cheek. "He seems to have lost his bearings momentarily."

"I heard that," I said from the open kitchen.

"He seems like a really nice man. I mean, to me," Winter said. "But they get a little strange sometimes, don't they?"

"Men?" Freddie said.

"The older ones. Young people scare them. My stepfather's been like that since I was ten."

"He still likes you, though," I said, coming back to the living room. "Cruel as you may be. And Winter is such a pretty name."

"I wish it was Batgirl," she said.

"Good choice," Freddie said.

"I'm going to watch the sunset," Winter said, getting up. "You guys want to see it?"

"Maybe in a bit," Freddie said. "I've got to put stuff away."

I followed Freddie into her bedroom. The light from outside the house was shadowy gold. There was a lot of racket out there—boom boxes and kids. Freddie had her backpack open, its contents strewn. She was pulling this stuff out—extra shoes, a tangerine, a rosary, a couple of New Age books, five white T-shirts—she had all this stuff stacked on the bed. She studied the work, replaced two things in her pack, put the rest in her closet. Then she went to the window and scissored open the blinds. I looked, too. Winter sat in a colored metal chair on the porch, drank beer, watched the light redden and fade. A dozen kids on bicycles circled the yard, cutting through the lot and driveway to do tricks in the street. They rode happily in circles. They had playing cards attached to their bikes with clothespins. The cards clapped as they circled the yard. The music just seemed to get louder.

"How was last night?" she said.

"Fine," I said. "Good."

The kids skidded their bikes, doing stunts and kicking up sand in the yard. We watched them in the twilight. The Mexican music was everywhere. Freddie traced the gaps between the knuckles on my hand. We stayed at the window listening to the music and the laughter, the taunts, cracks from the kids, the flapping cards, squeaking brakes—a slow-motion parade on this sandy Mississippi street, caught up in the dusk. A pretty thing.

17

I didn't want to make a habit of spending nights at Freddie's, so I stayed pretty close to home for the next week or so. I taught my classes, spent too much time in committee meetings, and generally kept a low profile, so I hadn't been following the adventures of Victor, whatever they were. Then Freddie called one night at eight-thirty. I was resting in bed, reading a new copy of *Bon Appetit*. Freddie was upset because Victor had gotten in some kind of jam in Memphis and needed help. He'd called Furlong, who couldn't be bothered, and then he'd called Winter, got Freddie. The story was that Victor was out of the hospital, but badly beaten, from what she could piece together. She wanted to know if I would drive up there with them to get him. "Winter's here, ready to go," she said.

"Memphis? How far is that? Can't he take a bus? Can't we just rent him a car?"

"Winter wants to go fetch. She's ready now, if you get my drift."

"The three of us?"

"Got our driving gloves on," Freddie said. "Everything I can do to keep her here now. We're in split second mode."

"Got it," I said.

"So?" she said. "I know your rooms are so lovely, you're so comfortable there, but she is, after all, your daughter, and she's ready to go."

"My room is very serene," I said. "But I am on my way."

I made a Blockbuster run en route to Freddie's, returning a couple of overdue Japanese videos, and when I got back in the car, the cell phone went off. It was Freddie. Winter had taken her car.

"She has a key," Freddie said. "She wants us to follow her. She'll go up Highway 49."

"I'm supposed to cut her off?" I said, twisting the wheel for a U-turn on the beach road.

"She can't have gone very far."

I made it to 49, the highway heading north. It wasn't long before I found Winter in a bright gas station that had a small silver-white blimp heliumed off it. This was a mile past the cloverleaf at 49 and I-10.

I called Freddie and said I'd found her. "I'll call back if I need you," I said.

I snapped the phone closed and stared out the windshield as Winter sat in Freddie's car intent on fiddling with something in her lap. I waited a minute and then pulled up at the pump next to her.

"We meet again," I said.

"Jesus! You scared shit out of me," she said. "You caught me."

"Well, yeah. What're you doing?" I got out of the car.

"Running away to, like, Memphis."

"Never been there," I said.

She surveyed the gas station. "I always end up in gas stations, you know. I like 'em. They smell good." She slid out of the car and circled around to my pump. "Some guy in a tuxedo was following me a minute ago. He's over there." She pointed across the street where there was an abandoned K-Mart store.

"I don't want to crowd you," I said.

"Yeah, well. Don't," she said. "You're here to stop me going to Memphis?"

"No," I said. "Catch you. We'll all go."

"Yeah?"

"Yeah, we'll go together." I was having some trouble with the gas pump. I stuck my card in and pulled it out fast, but the pump didn't read the card.

"Other way around," Winter said, pointing to the card, circling her forefinger.

I flipped the card and plugged it into the pump. It worked this time.

"Tonight?" she said.

"Now," I said. I fiddled with the nozzle, looked off toward the street. I must have looked as if somebody caught me in their headlights.

Winter said, "Cool," and put her arm around my shoulders while I held the nozzle in the gas tank. The pump beside us was chug-a-lugging as the gas came through and the counters spun.

"You don't want to think on this?" I asked. "Talk in the morning?"

"Gotta go now," she said. "The heart kinda calls." She dropped her forehead onto my shoulder. "I kind of need to do this."

"That's fine. I understand that. I'll gas up, and we'll go in my car—that O.K.?"

She gave me a small kiss on the cheek. "You're not bad, El. You could be way worse. Really."

"It's the gas station," I said. "Fumes. The horsy sound of the pumps. It slays the girls. I can't miss."

"In your element," she said.

When we left the gas station, I led the way, Winter followed. As we passed the video store, I grabbed the phone, punched redial, waited.

"Hello?" Freddie said.

"I got her. We're coming in." I checked the rearview to make sure she was still with me. "Listen, we need to go tonight. I told her we would."

"You're taking her to Memphis?"

"*We're,*" I said.

"Oh. O.K. Great," Freddie said. "I'll brush my teeth. It takes what, a month?

"Something like that," I said. "I don't want to go all that much."

"It's a really hard life," she said.

18

At three in the morning, the Memphis bus station was other-worldly, steamy, like an old Godard movie, that early one with Michael Constantine as the reporter gone to another planet, only the planet is really some Paris commercial district at night, office buildings and such, lots of empty sterile spaces finished in veneers and aluminum and mirrored glass. In the movie, all the people who drift through these spaces are elegantly dressed, as if just coming from a ritzy penthouse party of some kind, whereas in Memphis the dress code was more casual. Lots of pants held up with ropes. And there was plenty of Frenchness in the movie that wasn't quite present in the Memphis bus station. In fact, the more you looked at the Memphis bus station, the less it looked like any Godard movie, or any French movie, or anything French at all. It was pretty empty except for fat guys in uniforms with keys on retractable pull chains on their belts. Outside the street was steaming. Winter and Freddie were standing by a bus with DALLAS in the destination window. An assortment of bus freaks loitered. At some distance, Victor smoked a cigarette under a flickering neon sign.

"He doesn't look too beat up to me," I said.

"It's a detail," Freddie said.

"So why'd he leave his stuff here?" I asked.

"Didn't know how things were gonna turn out," Winter said.

"How *would* he know?" Freddie said.

A guy in a cap brought a couple of bags and checked some papers Victor handed over. I watched the silhouettes in the bus windows, sort of surprised everything was going my way. I was thinking, too, that I wouldn't mind being on the Dallas bus, or any other bus, rumbling out of the station. Land yacht, was the way I was thinking.

"Maybe we'll slip down to the Keys," Winter said to Freddie. "I mean, you know. After everything at home settles out some. Victor loves the Keys."

"Everybody loves the Keys," I said. "They're skinny."

A few minutes later we were tooling though downtown Memphis, Freddie and me in front, Victor and Winter in the back. Why we had to go in the middle of the night was anyone's guess, but I wasn't being choosy. Victor and Winter were whispering. The buildings were old. Freddie stared out the glass on her side of the car.

"This is a trick, Freddie. I know that," I said.

"You got it, Elroy."

Winter leaned over the seat. "Hey, Elroy?"

"What, dear?" I said.

"Uh, you know—what about a side trip? Huh?"

"To the casinos or something?"

"No, I was thinking we could spin over to Dallas for a minute."

"What?"

"It's not that far, is it?"

"Well, it isn't close," I said. "It's way over there." I pointed out Freddie's window.

I checked the rearview and watched Victor noisily leaf through a road atlas. I watched his little flashlight. Then he clicked on the dome light. "Only four hundred miles," he said.

"I've never been to Dallas," Winter said.

"Uh-huh," I said.

Winter slid back in her seat. She and Victor whispered and slapped at each other like kids.

"Hey, chill, youngsters," Freddie said. "Can't you people behave?" She curled more, eyed me from her side of the car, her head against the glass.

Victor and Winter were giggling, forehead to forehead. I snapped Freddie's leg with a couple of fingers, jerked my head toward the back. "They want to go to Dallas," I said.

"Winter's never been," she said.

———

We got onto North Danny Thomas Boulevard, then hooked up with I-40. It seemed to please Freddie, which pleased me. Winter and Victor were happy together in the backseat. A lot of nameless towns just flew right by in the middle of the night. We stopped a couple of times at gas stations stuck out by the highway. Near dawn everyone in the car was asleep, and I pulled in behind a strip mall somewhere short of Little Rock, parked it, and got some sleep myself. After that, we all cleaned up at the Wal-Mart and then did some shopping. There was a radio-controlled car place in the adjacent strip center, so naturally we had to stop there. Victor used to race, he told us. It was close to noon when we got back on the highway.

We got three more hours of driving in before everybody started getting cranky, so we stopped at some roadside place for a long lunch. Afterward, Winter and Victor took a walk down by a little river. Freddie and I stayed in the restaurant and got extra pie. About five, we were ready to take off again. All the cars stayed the same distance away from each other, moving at an easy pace. It took another three hours before we sailed under the huge "Welcome to Dallas" sign, and it was night already, so the city was all lit up. Somebody told them in Dallas that it was groovy to outline their buildings with lights, so they did. I parked on the street just a bit down from the front of the Hi-Lite motel.

"This is so cool!" Winter said, revived by the idea of sleeping in a bed, I guessed.

"The motel?" Victor said, slumping further in the backseat.

"Dallas," she said.

"My father was an assassination guy," Victor said. "My second father. He was here when it happened. I've seen that Zapruder film and those other films a thousand times. He even had the CD. A couple of CDs, really. Like games."

"Seen those," Winter said. "Those suck, really."

We opened some car doors while we collected ourselves after the drive.

"He made a model of every great national tragedy in his lifetime so far," Victor said. "When that rocket blew up, the Oklahoma deal, when they burned out that cult, you know? The World Trade Center—I mean, modeling was his deal, his whole deal, before his hands went. Well, I didn't see that last one, but like I heard about it, you know? He sent me pictures of it, of his version. When I was a kid it was mostly the JFK killing—he talked about it day in, day out," he said. "We had a model of the whole place, little tiny park thing, railroad bridge, the buildings—he made 'em all, painted 'em, had the cars, the limousines, the crowds. Tabletop model. I used to watch him move the cars around. He'd drink and move the cars around."

Victor and Winter slid out of the car. Freddie and I got out and went around to the trunk. "You O.K.?" I said to Winter.

"Fine," she said. "It's just a little . . . close in there."

"I'll take a turn in back if you want," Freddie said.

"So, what's his theory?" I said. "How many gunmen?"

"Who remembers?" Victor said. "All I remember is how he loved doing the gunfire. Ka-pow!" He held up his hands rifle-style, pointing at an imaginary target in the street. "Ka-pow! But then he moved on."

"Didn't we all," I said.

"Now, the Waco deal was harder, I think, 'cause mostly he saw it on TV, but I think he did all right with that one. I think I saw that one once, a few years ago. After a while the models got a little less detailed, you know? He wasn't sure what he'd seen at all. He wasn't much good. He was a drinking guy."

"So he was in the crowd for this Kennedy thing? In what, 1963 or something?"

"That's what he said," Victor said. "I don't know if I believe him. He used to lie about everything anyway. He was supposed to be a kid in the army. I don't really know, really. He wasn't my real father. He was this guy who hung around my mother all the time when I was growing up. He was always there. I guess he was my stepfather, but they never really got married. He could have been anybody."

"C'mon," Winter said. "He was your dad."

"He was a model guy. I mean, he made models. That's what he did for a living. I mean, when he made a living. He did it for insurance companies, for the cops and stuff. Killings and like that. Shoot-outs. Like they do now on TV reality shows—you've seen those things? He started all that, he was doing that for police all over the country. He was a strange guy my mom hooked up with.

Sometimes he just made little people and made them do stuff. He got a big kick out of that. He'd make a little family and a little house, and he put 'em through their paces. He loved that. Then my mom canned him."

"That happens," I said.

We hauled our suitcases toward the Hi-Lite's front door. In the street outside of the motel there was a hot dog vendor with one of those motor scooter carts. Victor waved him down, and then he and I ordered one apiece. We were the only ones who wanted anything.

Victor said, "Oswald was gay, anyway."

"He was?"

"Yeah, sure. Everybody knows that. That Selena thing, Martin, his wife, whatever that woman's name was, that was just a lie." He finished his dog and headed back for another.

We'd been on the road too long and we hadn't made good time, but I guessed that didn't matter. Winter took my arm as we walked into the Hi-Lite. Behind the motel registration counter there was a tiny man who wore a beat-up red suit and smoked a cigar. He was reading a J. Crew catalog. There was a fly swatter on the counter next to him.

"You the night man?" Victor said.

"Yeah, but I'm only half the man I used to be," the guy said. He didn't look up. The four of us exchanged a glance, like a ball ricocheting around the room.

"O.K., it's a movie," Winter said, pushing forward. "Let's get some rooms."

I had offered to put us up at a nice Holiday Inn, but there were no takers. The Hi-Lite had your standard-issue cheap-motel room—paneled walls, two double beds, an old beat-up RCA TV, and the obligatory seagull painting. Freddie was curled up on one of the beds in her room. She tried to flip TV channels but was having trouble with the remote. I was loitering.

"What the crap?" Freddie said.

"You O.K.?" I said.

She got an animal show on the screen, finally. "*Animal Planet.* Now I'm fine. Winter ought to stay in here with me. Where is she, anyway?"

"I *am* staying in here with you," Winter yelled from the bathroom.

"In the bathroom, I think," I said.

Freddie sat up in bed. "Victor can have a room by himself. I'll call Victor." She picked up the motel phone, started dialing.

I tried a chair, got up, pulled back the curtains, looked out at the brightly lit parking lot, started to close the curtains carefully, but they stuck. I inspected the curtain track, whipped the curtains back and forth, gave up, and took to the chair.

Winter's backpack was on the table, her stuff spilled out. The television was showing bears. Freddie got up and went into the shower. I started to follow, but Winter came out and said, "C'mon, Bub. Get lost here, will you? This is the girls' room."

I listened to the water splash around in the tub, moved toward the door, when Winter gave me a little shove. She shut her eyes. I called good-night to Freddie.

———

My room was dirty. I made the usual mistake of looking under the bed, looking in the corners of the room, looking at the bathtub. I don't know why I insist on this. You'd think I'd know better by now, but it always happens. You see stuff you don't want to see. In bad restaurants I'm always the guy who sees the little roach on the baseboard. Clare used to say that it was always the same roach. He traveled with us, she said. Not funny, McGee. Anyway, as soon as I got into my room at the Hi-Lite, I knew I was sleeping on top of the bed not in it, sleeping on a towel, using other towels to make a blanket. Always happens. I don't mind, and sometimes Clare said that I did it just because I wanted to play like I was Howard Hughes or somebody, that if I'd just relax I could crawl down in the dirt with everybody else and be perfectly happy. Who knows.

I called her and told her we were in Dallas. I told her we'd gone to Memphis to get Victor, and that Victor wasn't all fucked up like he was supposed to be, and that Victor and Winter wanted to go to Dallas, though it wasn't clear why. And I told her I was in my room on top of some towels, and she laughed and said, "You're always on top of something, Elroy." I didn't know what she meant, but I laughed because I've never known Clare to be mean-spirited, so maybe it was funny and I just didn't get it. Maybe she meant Freddie, but if she did, she meant it in the sweetest way.

I slept hard, and we all got a late start the next day. When I got up it was an hour past checkout. Winter and Victor had gone downtown to see the Dealey Plaza, which I thought everybody was finished with. But he had his father to think of. Freddie sweet-talked the desk person, and then we had lunch in the motel restaurant, which was fun. I had pancakes. Anytime you have pancakes for lunch, it's good for a lift. The waitress was pretty, too, in that waitress way.

It was afternoon when the four of us stood around the car at the BP station while I filled up with gas. My car leaned precariously over to one side.

"It's the shocks. Your shocks are gone," Victor said.

"Yeah?" I said.

"It's not shocks, Victor," Winter said. "Jesus. We've had this car a hundred years, and it's been leaning like this ever since I can remember. Maybe he bent the axle or something."

"Cars don't have axles anymore," Victor said. "You think there's like a pipe going across between the wheels?"

"They have little bitty axles, smart guy," Winter said, poking her forefinger out to represent an axle.

"The car's fine," I said. "It gets this way sometimes."

"It's tired?" Freddie said.

I rolled my eyes and stuck a credit card in the slot on the gas pump, withdrew it, got the nozzle, and started pumping gas. "You want to get it fixed? You *really* want to get it fixed? We can do that if you want. It'll slow us down."

"If we slow down any more, the tortoise'll blow on by," Victor said.

"Good one, Victor," Winter said.

"It's your party, Hoppy," I said.

"Let's just go," Freddie said.

I finished with the gas and capped the tank, returned the nozzle to the pump, waited for my receipt.

Winter studied the LCD display on the pump, "It says 'Thank you for shopping with us. Come back soon. Jesus died for your sins.' Really—*Jesus died for your sins.*"

"I heard that," Freddie said.

"Man, we ought to burn this place," Victor said. "We ought to crash it hard with the car. Man, that's blasphemy."

"Yeah," Freddie said. "We need to stand up for our God-given right to gas up without being attacked by Jesus."

"Sheesh, what's with Mrs. Dodo?" Winter said, climbing back into the car. "She's no fun."

The receipt got stuck up in the slot. Freddie bumped her head against window glass climbing into the car. Winter whispered to Victor, and then Victor got her in a headlock in the backseat. I could see it was going to be my big day.

We rolled back onto the highway. The landscape was flat and green. The sky was gourami blue.

————

Freddie drove for a while, then we switched, but everybody was tired from the night before, so we quit early, just past Shreveport in a town called Rubric, Louisiana. Victor took his suitcase and headed for the men's room at the Pilot House Restaurant, while the three of us sat around a table chockablock with pies, pastries, French fries, and coffee.

"What's with him?" I said to Winter. Everybody was busy eating.

"The Memphis trip bummed him," she said.

"What exactly happened?"

"Don't know,"Winter said, still staring at the Pilot House menu. "Your friend Edward would have loved this place, wouldn't he?"

I looked around. "I suppose. Why?"

"He would have," she said. "I only met him a couple times, but I'll bet."

"She's right," Freddie said. "He'd have been shooting video every which a way. He would have loved that gecko farm we passed back there. Who could find that to do, you know, in life?"

"Some people are so wonderful in this world,"Winter said.

Victor came back wearing a cheap black suit that didn't fit so well. He looked uncomfortable. He'd colored his hair a red-black, black with red highlights. He had a leather-bound Bible with gold-edged pages in his hand, and he slapped it down on the table with authority.

"I feel better now," he said.

"Great," Winter said. "What'd you do to your hair? You dye your hair? In the men's room?"

"Never can tell when you're going to run into somebody," he said. "You're there, wherever, doing whatever, and bang! Furlong shows up out of nowhere, and that's the whole thing right there."

"The whole thing what?" she said.

"Why I rode that bus to Memphis," he said. "I used to travel with the guy. We were going everywhere together. I shouldn't let it get to me," he said. "He wanted to go to Graceland. I'd ridden all over the country on the buses, and here he comes with the big car. Wherever it is, I been there. So he comes up and says, 'You going to see Elvis?' And I say, 'I don't mind.' I mean, he's kinda repellent. Not to mention the toilet."

"Pigboy," Freddie said.

"I thought you liked Elvis," Winter said.

"You take the tour and you get to see," Victor said. "I mean, if people come all the way across this great land of ours to see a toilet, well, I don't know. Something's fucked." He slid a holy card in the Bible to mark a spot and then reclosed the book. "We were going together, didn't matter where," he said.

"My Furlong?" Winter said.

"Yeah. In his big Cadillac, streaming along," Victor said, floating his hand out over the tabletop. "You know, when you travel across country you ought to see something breathtaking."

"Got that right," Freddie said, swapping pies with him.

He pulled out a manila envelope with photographs and travel pamphlets, maps carefully plotted, written on, annotated, detailed. Suddenly the booth seemed filled to overflowing with his paraphernalia. He was a travel agent all of the sudden.

I was kind of derailed, not paying that much attention. I wanted to retire and sit deadpan in front of a television for a while. See what was on. Some murder show or a forensic show where they put the bones back together twenty years later, or maybe something on E! set in an international hot spot. Everybody is so oily in those shows, but the girls have that foreign look to them. They're not as good as the girls in the Anthropologie catalog, but they're close.

"You got to know these things," he said. "Now, there's a bridge right about here—" he tapped the map somewhere in the Mississippi Delta, "—it's over a little creek. They say the creek isn't but about thirty-five feet wide, but there's this trestle bridge that the train crosses every night about sunset." He had two or three pages in his hand and was pointing out this spot close to the Tennessee/Mississippi border. "It's outside a town called Mondrian. Then I was going to drift down here—" he dragged a little finger south, "—to Soso, Hot Coffee, Peanut, just because they're there. That was my itinerary."

"Man, I ought to be traveling with you," Winter said.

"Well, you kinda are," Victor said.

My chicken-fried steak was smothered in white gravy. I picked at it, licking gravy off the tines of the fork. I watched my reflection in tall doors that opened out onto the Pilot House patio. From the next room I heard snatches of dialogue between two TV commentators who were talking about morality. One guy was saying that the public contract with the American people was to uphold the fundamental tenets of decency, honesty, and morality, and the other guy was saying that he couldn't agree more.

I stopped playing with my food.

———

We got rooms for the night at the Pine Tree Motor Lodge, a brown wood building next to the restaurant, low and stretched down toward some dried out pond at the edge of the parking lot. The Pine Tree was awful from the outside but clean as could be inside. Everyone took a nap, and then we reconvened on the second floor balcony of Freddie and Winter's room. They were smoking cigarettes, drinking Mexican beer. I was watching the traffic on the interstate. Victor was hulking around, in a small way.

"I was thinking about your father," Freddie said. "Like with his models, and I was trying to imagine what that must've been like."

"Stepfather," Victor said. "Something. I don't even know what you'd call it."

"I was thinking about him in your house—"

"Trailer. It was a trailer," Victor said.

Freddie illustrated, drawing in the air. "I could see him working on that World Trade Center thing, moving those airplanes, swishing them in there like they did, and the smoke and fire, and the little tiny people jumping out the windows on the ninetieth floor and stuff. Man, that was the worst part. Little tiny screams. I mean, think about that—what's with that? Edward's got a lot of that video. He must have watched a lot of that."

"Like fleas," Winter said. "That's what it looked like."

"I try to imagine it," Freddie said. "Out there in the air like that, flying down, what the sound was, fear exploding your fucking head."

"Ka-pow," Winter said.

Headlights of passing cars played on the street signs and trees and the buildings that lined the highway.

"I wonder what it would have been like to see your father when he was really interested, seeing his obsessions up close. That would be something," Freddie said.

"He was just a guy," Victor said. "That's the part I liked. I mean, everybody is, in the end. Thomas Jefferson, Adam Clayton Powell, everybody."

Winter shot a cigarette out into the parking lot and lit up a new one. She pumped the ashes of the new one to a bright fire, her face lit up by the burn. "I should take a walk," she said.

"Want company?" I said.

"No," she said.

Victor said, "My dad was loony, but I guess he could've been worse." He got up and opened the sliding door. "I'm checking my room," he said.

"Yeah, well," Freddie said. "Fathers are hard."

"But you miss 'em when they're gone," I said.

"I hear that," Winter said. She took a drag and blew smoke elaborately out her nose—a practiced thing.

"So, what were you like when I was a kid?" Winter said, squinting at me.

"I was an art guy," I said. "I did art. I didn't pay much attention to you. You were little and spoiled."

"No way," Winter said.

"Sorry," I said. "True is true."

"No, listen," Winter said, holding her hand out as if she was stopping everything to tell some story. "He was a local hero. The brooding artist. Always in the paper being interviewed about his art shows, scaring everybody with crazy art things. He made pieces out of tire tubes, water hoses, beds. We used to have this big book of his clippings from the *Times-Picayune,* some paper in New York, the *Sun-Herald*—lots of them. I learned to read reading newspaper stories about him."

"That right?" Freddie said.

"Oh yeah. I was hot, all right," I said. "I read a lot of magazines in those days."

"You were probably great," Freddie said. "You probably did all the stuff before everybody else did it, right? There are people like that everywhere. They get there first, they move on."

"I did some of that," I said.

"He was like rain," Winter said. "When you need rain."

They stopped and stared at each other, and then Freddie reached out and swatted Winter's bare arm. "Girl . . . ," she said.

They laughed a minute.

"I *was* like rain," I said. "Exactly."

Freddie said, "Now, too." She bummed a hit off Winter's beer. Bummed a cigarette.

"Uh-oh," Winter said. "Naw, he's kind of a trash dog, isn't he? He drives all around with us when we're going nowhere. He's a Noble Furlong kind of guy, only the good version."

"What's that even mean?" Freddie said.

"I don't know," Winter said. "I just said it."

"Maybe I ought to step out for a while," I said. "So you guys can have some privacy."

"We don't *need* no privacy, Elroy," Freddie said. "We got all we want. What we need is you shave twenty years off the resume, know what I mean?" She stood and tossed her beer bottle at a Dumpster on the ground below. Hit it dead center. "You just sit there and see if you can time travel back to us, O.K.?"

Freddie and Winter went inside, and I waited a couple minutes, then I went in, too, sat on one of the beds and started switching the television. Winter tapped my head as she went by, heading out the motel room door. "I'm sorry, Bozo. I didn't mean it. I mean, I meant it, but you're cool just the way you are." She pointed at the door she was walking toward. "I'm checking on Victor."

"So the whole deal is he just wanted you to come to Memphis?" I said. "I hate to ask, but I'm just checking."

Winter and Freddie exchanged a look. "Yes, Paw-Paw," Winter said. "It were a ruse." She stopped in the door. "You're not going to hold it against him, are you?"

"Might," I said.

She shook her head, let the door latch behind her.

Freddie stood alongside me a minute watching the TV, then gathered her things and said, "I'm going to clean up."

"Maybe I'll stick around for a bit," I said.

"Help yourself."

She went into the bathroom and locked the door. I cycled through the channels, settling eventually for the home and garden channel, where some buzz-haired guy was helping a fat woman turn her tiny garden into a sunken outdoor patio dining site. He dug a hole in the garden and poured some concrete, then put a glass top on a pedestal in the hole and some cushions around the hole. It didn't take much to figure how that was going to look after a couple of months.

After her shower, Freddie came out and sat on the second bed, filed her nails, smoked, and occasionally glanced at the television. There was a knock. She and I did a look, and then I went to answer. It was Victor.

"You seen Winter?" he said.

"No," I said. "She went to find you."

We stood in the open door. Freddie got off the bed and joined us. "She went out. About a half hour ago. She's probably just taking a walk or something."

"I'll check the parking lot," Victor said.

"I should go, too," Freddie said.

Victor stopped at the door. "No, that's O.K. I'll get her."

He left, and I closed the door. It made a heavy thunk. I turned and Freddie caught me in the little hallway outside the bathroom, pushed me against the wall, started to kiss me.

When you haven't kissed somebody in a while, and you want to, it's very intense, even the simplest kiss. That's the way this was. I was thinking she probably didn't want to do much of it, so I was on the lookout for any sign of her pulling away. That sign arrived sooner than I would have liked, so I let it go and she went back to the bed.

"I'm going to help Victor," I said.

"Fine," she said, staring at the TV remote, trying to find the buttons she wanted.

I went downstairs and found Victor wandering in the Pine Tree's lot as if he were lost. It was a good-sized lot, ribboned with cars.

"Any luck?"

"I asked the night guy, but he hadn't seen her," Victor said.

In a few minutes Freddie showed up outside, too. "Winter's up in the room. What are you guys doing?"

"It's a play." I said.

The three of us stood in the eerily lit parking lot for a few seconds. Bugs were zipping around. I started for the lobby. "Maybe I'll get a drink."

"I'm turning in," Victor said. "See you tomorrow."

Freddie followed me into the bar. The bar was dark and empty. "She's been feeling claustrophobic," Freddie said. "A little too much Victor, I think. He doesn't get it."

"Good news," I said.

"He's not so bad. Pretty map orientated."

"Uh-huh," I said. "You O.K.? You look tense."

"I'm dandy."

I just stared at her. I couldn't think of what to say. There were so many things that were possible to say, but none of them seemed the right thing to say, and I was sort of lost about what to do, so I didn't do anything for a minute or two, just sat there, looking at her, and what I wondered was what she thought she was doing—what she thought we were doing—at this dive in the middle of Louisiana. I just thought it would be great to be inside somebody else's head for a while, to hear the noise in there.

Finally I said, "You know how parents always smell a certain way? When you hug them and—you know? They smell this certain way? That's something amazing."

19

We were up at noon having breakfast at the Pilot House. Then Victor wanted to "walk the town," as he put it, so he and Winter and Freddie took off. I went to an ancient Walgreen's drugstore and looked at some dusty postcards and then went back to the motel to call the school and get somebody to cover my classes for the rest of the week.

By mid-afternoon everyone was tired again. We checked out and climbed into the car like bears. I steered us back onto the highway, and in no time all, three of them were asleep in the backseat, tumbled over each other. Heading southeast across Louisiana, having just come out of Texas, you got a good idea what water could do for land. It was lush and creepy, about the prettiest magic forest stage set you could imagine.

I looked into the rearview, craning my head to see what was going on in the back.

Freddie caught me, sat up, and unfolded a map. "Where are we?"

"Headed home," I said.

"Why are you staring back here? What do you see?"

"Three little pigs?"

She grimaced, refolded the map, lit a cigarette, passed it over the back of the seat to me. "Knock yourself out," she said.

I took the cigarette and held it between my thumb and forefinger, switched my eyes back and forth between the smoke and the highway. I didn't smoke very often. When I did, it brought back another world, another life. I was there, remembering that, when Freddie climbed over the seat back and took up her post on the passenger side. She retrieved the cigarette, then plopped the visor down, and went to work righting her makeup.

"I think I'm going to hang around, maybe do the degree thing," she said. "That O.K. with you?"

"Fine," I said.

"Getting a degree never hurt," she said. "Well, except Edward." She fingered the radio buttons, punching every one but the On/Off. "I think Edward was sweeter on me than I really knew. I sure wasn't ready for this."

"You couldn't have been," I said.

We were flying through afternoon shadows. It was wall-to-wall green out there. Lots of stuff leaning over other stuff, making sure that everyone understood that fertility was Job One. I was worried about what she was telling me, what she wanted me to hear, worried that we were getting to the point at which one of us was going to feel it necessary to make some pronouncements. I hate that kind of thing. I like to simmer, just coast along and adjust course little by little, but maybe it was a mess for her, and she needed clarity. I was trying to send her a telepathic message to change the subject when she motored right on through.

"You going to be O.K. if I'm there?" Freddie said.

"You mean . . . what? In school? Sure. We can be like, you know, whatever. Go to dinner. You can come watch the fights on TV. Be great."

"I'd like that," she said.

"Wash my plates," I said.

"*Now* you're talking," she said.

I checked the rearview. For my trouble I got a stare out of Victor, who looked as if he'd been caught listening in. He held my eyes for a second, and then said, "Still here. Still watching."

"Good. Thanks. Maybe you could watch my darling step-daughter for a while?"

"I am *in* the house," Victor said. "But I thought that'd be about last on your list."

"You resist for a while," I said. "Then you let it go."

I looked away from the mirror, then back. He did a half-hearted wave that meant something friendly and turned to stare out the car window.

Freddie handed the cigarette to me. I brought it to my face and stopped, studied the filter. There was a red lip print on the end of the cigarette. I put it in my mouth, gently closing on the filter with my lips, then pulling them away, tasting the lip gloss, feeling the skin of my lips stick.

Victor reached over the front seat and plucked the map away from Freddie, then started arranging it, folding and refolding, smoothing it. The map crackled as he worked.

I turned to Freddie. "Is Victor taking a new position, or is that my imagination?"

"We have a day to go, Victor," she said. "We can't make it tonight."

"Got a late start," I said.

From behind the map Victor said, "You don't have to worry about me."

I tapped the button Freddie had skipped, then tapped it again, and then hit the electronic tuning until some station came in playing Hawaiian music.

"Perfect," Victor said.

Four identical Ford pickups went by us on the highway, all of them black, with dark windows, wearing Vermont tags, each with *Bombay Slaughter* on the door. Freddie watched them go and then turned to look out the back window to see if there were more.

"Are we being followed?" she said. "What's up?"

Victor folded the map down, sighed heavily. "Nobody back here but us chickens," he said.

———

Two hundred miles south, somewhere just shy of Opelousas, we stopped at a giant no-name gas station with a half-acre of oyster shell parking lot, some diesel tanks on one side, and a sloppy-looking diner attached to the store. I pulled under the overhang next to a set of yellow pumps.

Winter, who'd been sleeping on and off the whole trip, woke up with her hair like crazy spider legs. She said. "Where are we?"

"Getting there," Freddie said. "How're you feeling?"

"Better. I have to pee."

"I'll go with," Freddie said.

They crossed the shell lot and went into the store. A minute later they were back out with a green key on a string that was attached to a large pie tin. They headed around back.

Victor and I were at the gas pumps. Victor was doing some elaborate stretches while I pumped gas. Victor said, "I don't want to be forward or anything, but aren't you a little old for this? I mean, Freddie and all that?"

"I am, Vic. I am Mr. Warmed Over."

We watched Freddie and Winter come back around the building and go back into the convenience store. "But seriously," he said. "What is with you and her?"

"Well, Victor, I don't know if this is in your bailiwick. You know what a bailiwick is? Well, you have one, and this isn't in it."

"Ah, c'mon," he said. "Be a pal."

"We're like friends or something. It's not a violation of natural law."

"O.K.," he said, shaking his mop. "We're in worse shape here than I thought."

I looked around at the landscape. Everything out there was kind of like Sal Mineo's hair, if you remember Sal Mineo's hair, but made out of plants and multiplied a million times and coming up and spilling over his forehead in a hundred directions. Pines, oaks, sixty kinds of green weeds, lots of shade. There was a creek off to the side, and a guy was selling fruit out of a pickup.

"If you keep your covenant with me," Victor said, "I will give you rain in its season."

"Covenant," I said.

"Like a promise. You know what a promise is?"

"I do indeed," I said.

I finished with the gas, and we went inside to see what was holding up the women. Ten seconds after we hit the door, we were face down on the concrete floor right alongside them, plus the woman cashier, an old farmer, and a dog. Two guys in Lone Ranger masks—one with a mechanical left hand and the other a Hispanic kid with elaborate facial hair—stood over us pointing small guns.

The hand guy said, "Just don't do anything. Nobody do nothing. O.K.?"

The second guy said, "Get the register. I'll watch them."

The first guy waved his mechanical hand and said, "Maybe you better do it, huh?"

"Oh, yeah. Right," the Latin kid said. He went behind the counter, started slapping the buttons on the register.

"It's the blue one. The big blue one," the cashier said.

"Thank you, ma'am," the hand guy said. He turned to the kid. "The blue button. Do the blue button."

"I've got two buttons. Light blue, dark blue," the Latin said.

"Bright blue," the cashier said.

I was next to Winter. I reached for her arm, gave her a reassuring touch. "Just do what they say. It'll be fine," I whispered.

She jerked away from me. "Quit. Quit touching."

The guy with the hand fired his pistol into a stack of soup cans on a shelf behind us. Liquid squirted out.

The dog growled, low and quiet, but unrelenting.

"You Dumb and Dumber?" the hand guy said. "Keep your mouth shut, face down, watch the concrete."

"Reach for the sky," Victor whispered.

"What's that?" the hand guy said, but he couldn't figure out who'd said it, me or Victor. I was ready to tell him when he turned to the Latin kid, "Got it yet?" He walked around us on the floor and used his mechanical hand to pick up a soup can with a hole in it.

"Yeah, yeah, I got it," the kid said.

"How much?"

"Couple hundred."

The hand guy said, "Try the restaurant."

The Hispanic stuffed the cash from the register into his pocket and headed into the restaurant. The hand guy drizzled soup on my shirt. "Here you go, pal. How about some Progresso?"

"Do the rest, why don't you?" Winter said. "Those people are slag."

"Lookee here," the guy said. "An activist! Kind of small scale from the look of you. Or maybe you just talk about *your causes,* huh? From time to time? When it suits you? When somebody's listening, and you think maybe they'll be impressed that you worked hard on the Chiquita banana thing?" He started moving down the line to her.

Suddenly there was screaming from the restaurant, then three shots. Snappy sounding, like a pellet gun.

The hand guy dropped the soup can and went to the restaurant door. His buddy came out more or less carrying a waitress as if he'd been dancing with her forty-eight hours straight. She was young and she was in uniform and she was bleeding.

"What in the fuck are you doing?" the hand guy said.

"I didn't kill her," the kid said.

"Congratulations."

"You *almost* killed me," the waitress said. "You shot me."

"She came out of nowhere," the Hispanic said.

"Let's go, Mouse," the older guy said.

The Hispanic whirled around as if to slug his partner. "Don't call me that. Don't ever call me that." He waved his gun at the guy with the hand.

"O.K. All right. This is a good idea. You learn this at the Famous Robbers School?"

"I'm not kidding, man. Nobody calls me Mouse no more," the kid said.

"Fine," he said. "Can we leave?"

I sat up, tried to clean off my shirt with some paper towels that had been knocked on the floor.

"Don't worry about that, you fuck," the hand guy said.

"I'm down, I'm down!" I said, getting face down on the floor again.

The dog watched everything, still growling, and the old farmer said, "You hush now, Tonto."

"That dog's named Tonto?" the Latin kid said.

"Yes sir."

"Let's take him with us," the kid said to the older guy.

This was way too much. Using his mechanical hand, he flattened the kid, whose gun skittered across the floor and stopped right under my nose.

The dog stopped growling.

"Gun here," I said, lifting my head up and back, away from the pistol. "I ain't touching it. All yours."

The Latin kid was on the floor, bleeding from his ear, a cut from his partner's mechanical hand. He retrieved his gun and in a rage stuffed it in my face as if to shoot me.

This was the second time in my life I had been held at gunpoint. It is a very peculiar feeling, not at all like the movies. Things are terribly clear when someone has a gun pointed at you. It's a little hard to breathe. You look at the barrel, and it looks clean and the opening is dark, and you have this strange feeling of just how close you are to the edge of things, just a tiny movement of the finger and you're dead, or close to it. For that time it's like everything changes, and there's only this one thing in the world, these seconds with this gun pointed at you. They go by slow and clear. You think it won't happen, he won't pull the trigger, but then you think he could, just as easily as not. Maybe you look up at his eyes to see what you can see there, but they don't give much away, only that he doesn't have a clue about what's going to happen either. That's scary. Besides, you don't want to take your eyes off the barrel for long, so you look at the gun again. You see the space between the gun and you, and you have a new respect for space. You think how quick that bullet is going to fly across that space.

"You ever been shot, Gramps?" the kid said. "Huh?"

"No, sir. Mr. Mouse, sir," I said. This was wrong and I knew it was wrong and it could not have been more wrong. The tone was bad, the content was bad. I knew before it was all the way out.

The kid's face went into a giant grin. He swiveled to his right and fired a shot into Freddie's arm. She screamed, rolled, grabbed her arm, her face twisted up like Halloween.

Then the kid leaned in close to me, tapped my temple with his little gun barrel. "See there? Tell you what, now any time you want to know what it feels like you can just ask her, O.K.? Just ask."

He wiped the blood off his ear with his pistol hand and stepped over me, following his partner to the door.

We stayed on the ground a few minutes and then got up. The cashier called the police; I looked at Freddie's arm. Winter and the farmer tended to the waitress, who had been hit in the hip.

Victor sat cross-legged on the floor shaking his head. "Mr. Mouse," he said. "That's rich."

———

Victor and Winter sat across from me in the small emergency room at the local hospital. Through a little window to an operating room we watched a tiny nurse dressing Freddie's wound.

"I'm telling you," Winter said. "We never had this kind of trouble until we started hanging out with you."

"Thanks," I said. "You're a pal."

"Well, it's damn true," she said.

"Are you O.K.?" Victor asked her. "I was scared when you were gone last night."

"That's really sweet," she said.

Victor drew a line down the center of her face with his finger, starting at her forehead and going to the chin. "I need to divide you into parts so I can know you better."

Winter grabbed Victor's finger and said, "I'm not sure that's a good idea. You don't want to know me too well."

"Why?"

"Well, that kind of thing happens sometimes. I go off. It's like my hobby or something." She looked serious, as if she were telling him a truth. "I don't know why. I'm always going around on somebody."

Winter got up and started for the door, but Victor caught her wrist. "It's fine, we're finished here," she said.

"You're my hobby," he said. "How's that?"

"Try trains," Winter said.

"Fair warning," he said.

The nurse walked Freddie out into the waiting room, patting her arm. "Looks beautiful," the nurse said. "Never saw a more perfect gunshot wound. You're going to have a pretty little scar."

"What're you, high?" Freddie said.

The nurse laughed. "No, really. It'll be like a secret, like a hidden tattoo. Everybody needs a secret."

"I've got my share already. What I'm more worried about is, is it going to hurt?" Freddie gently smoothed the bandage over her arm.

"I'll give you a little slug of something. How's that?"

"You're the doctor," Freddie said.

I went outside while they settled up with the hospital. In the parking lot I started the car and twisted the AC to high, then slumped over the wheel and listened to the air conditioning. For a minute I had my head down on top of the steering wheel. Two young girls in cheerleader outfits walked by practicing a cheer.

I sat up and watched out the windshield as these two pranced by and then stepped out of the way as Freddie, Victor, and Winter came out of the hospital. They came across the lot, heading for the car. I stared at Freddie, and she looked so young.

When she got to the car, she clicked a ring on the window, signaled me to run the glass down. I did.

"Give me the cell," Freddie said.

"O.K." I handed the phone out the car window.

Winter and Victor opened the back doors of the car. Victor sat down on the edge of the seat and Winter stayed outside. Freddie dialed a number on the telephone, then stood by the front door of the car, looking at her bandaged arm.

"Clare?" I heard her say. "Hi. This is Freddie. Yeah. Look, we're late. We ran into some trouble. Well, I mean, everybody's O.K. Winter's fine and Elroy's fine. But, well—we just bumped into a convenience store robbery. Everybody's O.K.—" she pointed at the phone to ask me if I wanted to talk.

I shook my head.

"No, we're all fine," Freddie said. "We were going to get there today, but I think it's tomorrow now. You want to talk to Elroy?"

I wagged *No,* but Freddie whispered, "Quit that, you're going to hurt yourself," and handed the phone over. I bobbled it, but finally got it to my ear.

"Hey," I said.

Freddie lit a cigarette and gestured at me with it. "Tell everything. I'm serious."

"We're in Louisiana, close to Opelousas. We kind of got in the middle of a thing at this grocery store, and a kid shot her in the arm because I said something, I kind of made fun of him. It was just really stupid. Unforgivable." I signaled Freddie for another cigarette.

Winter came around the car, leaving Victor in the backseat.

"Tell her I jumped you in the motel room," Freddie said. "Tell her about the time in your office."

Winter did a take. "You did what?"

On the phone, Clare said, "What did she say?"

"Nothing," I said. "We're fine, things are going slow though. Winter's good."

"Jesus," Winter said. "I am getting bashed here. This some kind of *Temptation Island* deal?"

"Let me call you later," I said to Clare. "Everything's fine. We've got to make up some time tonight. We should be there by now, but, you know. Got off late, stopped in East LA."

"You sure Winter's all right?" Clare said.

"She's perfect," I said. "You want to talk to her?" I held the phone out to Winter, who was outside the passenger door window, smoking.

"Hi, Mom," I heard her say, moving away from the car.

Victor came around and stood with Freddie by the driver's door. He stared into the car at me. "Man, this has gone about as far as we need to go. I mean, let's drive it and get it over with."

"Chill, will you?" Freddie said.

I put my forehead back on the steering wheel.

Freddie leaned in, her hand on my shoulder, her face close to mine. "You O.K., Elroy ?"

"I'm good to go," I said.

20

We didn't get far, what with the police and the hospital and the fact that we'd started late to begin with. We made it down through Opelousas and Sunset and then went east at Lafayette on I-10 across the long bridge over the Atchafalaya, and just after we were over that we decided to call it a night in Pelba, a tiny, low spot just off the highway. Not even a town, really. We found a place called the Bayside Sleeper, which was a collection of single-story stucco cottages, dotted in among pines bordering the swamp. It was dark when we got there. It was a place like a hundred others; somebody in the forties had an idea to make a killing by throwing up these tiny shacks around a gravel lot off a highway. Only it was a different highway then, a different world. We got our bungalows and retired. I bathed and shaved and sat on the bed, looking at the fritzy television for a while, and then went outside to stretch my legs. The only light outside came from a couple of bare bulbs high in the trees. Freddie sat on a picnic table thirty yards from the cottages. She had on a sleeveless cotton top.

She waved me over. "Pretty nice out here," she said. She eased off the picnic table and linked arms with me and steered me toward the slip of water that curled behind the motel.

"How's the arm?"

"Good as new," she said. "Feels like somebody's been pounding on it with a screwdriver."

We crossed a small bridge to a bench that was in a clearing at the edge of the swamp. A couple old skiffs bobbed and banged against the pier. There was a big moon.

"I was waiting for you to come out," Freddie said. "I think we have to talk."

"We do?" I said.

"I mean, the deal with Edward was a shock," she said. "That kind of got me. But I'm coming back now. I'm ready to go on with stuff—school, everything."

"Uh-huh," I said. "Not much choice."

"You know what I mean," she said. "It's like, we're out here, and we've got all our stuff with us all the time, and it takes a while. It's not as simple as they make it on TV."

"You're losing me," I said. "What's not as simple?"

"Everything. And it's not even *about* the same stuff, is it? It's all so orderly on TV; people do stuff and say stuff and think stuff, and everything makes sense—it's as if we have this madness for things making sense. But they don't, do they? We can make them, but by themselves they don't."

"Well, that's one school of thought," I said.

"So I'm just a kid," she said. "I figure you either force things or you don't. You don't, do you?"

"I try," I said. "God knows I try."

"Quit," she said.

Something like a double-size pointy-nosed cat shuffled up on the bank maybe thirty feet to our right, shook itself, and then hunched up there, looking like a beaver-weasel-otter. "What's that?" I said.

"A living thing," Freddie said. "Looks like a beaver."

"Probably not a beaver," I said.

"Whatever," she said. "We better get moving." She pulled me to my feet. "C'mon. I'll take you for a drive."

"Been driving," I said.

She stopped by the hood of the car, lit one cigarette off another. As she smoked the new cigarette, she watched the ash on the old one. There were maybe twenty actual cats of various descriptions creeping around.

We got in and crunched out of the parking lot onto a two-lane road that ran parallel to I-10, then led us up onto the highway. We headed east. Pretty soon it was closing on two o'clock, and a steamy fog hung over the highway. Near an exit for a town called Wedgeville we ran across a partially lit Greyhound bus that was pulled off the road into some weeds. A truck was parked close to the back of the bus, and three guys were out there talking to the driver. The men stood in the truck's headlights, facing into the opened engine compartment of the bus. They pointed their flashlights around.

We pulled up behind the truck, and Freddie and I sat in our seats, eating cheese sandwiches we'd picked up at an all-night gas station. Some of the bus passengers were milling around on the side of the highway; some stayed in the bus so you could just see their heads through the bus windows.

"You want to get on this bus?" I said.

"What, you mean buy a ticket and everything?"

"Sure," I said. "Go where it goes."

"I don't see it," she said.

"Me either," I said. "Maybe back when." I crushed half a cheese sandwich into a ball and tossed it into the field by the roadside. "For birds," I said.

"We can go take a look," Freddie said. "Doesn't look like this bus is going anywhere anytime soon." She got out, and I followed her past the truck and alongside the bus. We waved greetings to the driver guy and his pals. At the front door Freddie climbed on and waved her sandwich at me motioning for me to follow.

The people on the bus were mostly asleep or reading or listening to earphones. They didn't pay attention to us. Freddie went into the bathroom on the bus but came out lickety split.

"Now *that's* no picnic," she said. "Let's get out of here."

We dropped off into weeds up to our knees. We walked along the side of the bus away from the highway. The truck's headlights haloed the back where the driver was closing up his cell phone.

"What's it look like?" Freddie said.

"Looks like a moment under the stars," the guy said, apparently figuring us for his passengers.

Freddie and I looked at the sky. The fog was way too thick—there was no sky.

"How long?" she said.

"Hour," he said. "Can you stand it?"

"We're taking a walk," Freddie said, leading me into the weeds.

"Not too far," the bus driver said.

She waved at him without turning around. "You'd think he'd notice, wouldn't you?" she said.

"Hard to see out here," I said. "Where're we headed?"

"Tree line," she said, climbing a short embankment. "We can see everything from up there."

———

Fifty minutes later we were on the ground in a clearing maybe a hundred yards from the bus, pleasantly disheveled and smoking cigarettes, leaning up against trees. I still had my shirt on. She fiddled with the buttons. In the distance, the guys were finishing up with the Greyhound.

"Well, who knew?" she said. "And we're a classy bunch, you and me. Out here in the woods—it's nice. You're a young man, after all. You screw like a monkey."

"Yes?" I said. "Well—thank you. That's something."

She sighed, whisked a little spot in front of her with a pine twig. "I guess sometimes the hard-as-nails thing isn't quite the deal."

I watched the lazy cigarette smoke coil and rise in front of me. "It wasn't bad, dear."

She reached for my bare foot and twisted it a little. "It was fucking fabulous."

The way this made me shiver was embarrassing. My neck muscles contracted, then released. I was working pretty close to the surface. "Maybe you could *whisper* that?" I said.

"Anytime," she said, patting the foot. "But now we've got to go back, sleep. Tomorrow we start again, we go home, we do right."

There was a commotion around the bus. Men laughed, and the engine compartment of the bus shut with a bang, and then there was a loud burst on the bus horn.

I looked over, and the driver was on the steps craning his head looking for passengers. Some other passengers inside the bus lined up behind him.

"All aboard! Anybody out there?" the driver yelled.

We sat still there in our little clearing, watched as the driver corralled his people, got everybody back inside, said goodbye to the guys from the truck and some other people that had come up without us noticing. In a few minutes the bus bled off the air brakes and pulled back into the fog. Trucks followed, and then there was only our car there on the side of the road.

Freddie tugged at my shirt, straightened herself out, and we walked hand in hand through the tall wet weeds. The highway glowed. Cars fizzed by.

———

Outside the Bayside Sleeper, the morning light was way too bright. The motel was worse off in daylight. On the other side of a stand of trees, a couple of kids in boxer swimsuits did cannonballs and jackknives off a diving platform into the middle of an above-ground pool.

We left our cottage doors open while we put the luggage in the car.

"We're not taking all day to do this either," Winter said, hauling her backpack to the car.

I lofted my suitcase into the trunk. "Take it easy. We'll get there soon enough."

"I'm sure," she said. She slapped at me on her way into Victor's cottage. "Unless the trip continues the way it's been going. Did you plan this? Drive an hour and then get a hotel? Is that some old duck's strategy?"

"He drives like a Chinaman," Freddie said, smiling.

"I like to drive it straight through," I said. "Me, personally."

"Whoa," she said.

"You want me to drive?" Victor said to me.

"No, I got it."

We got in the car. It rocked a bit as we readied ourselves for travel. I worked on my seat belt. Winter and Victor moved stuff around in the backseat. Freddie looked at a map.

All the cats from last night were visible, scattered around in groups of two, three, and four. They perched on the roofs of the cottages, on the lower limbs of the trees, underneath the porches, watching us get ready.

———

Everyone was quiet. We rolled through Baton Rouge and on to Hammond and Slidell. Once, traveling at highway speed, I started to take a weedy turn off that led into a gas station and restaurant called Buster's One Stop, but Freddie grabbed for the steering wheel, swerving the car onto the shoulder of the road and then back up onto the highway, kicking up a lot of dust and rocks.

"Not on your life, motherfucker," she said. "Exxon, BP, Shell. Period. I don't care what they're doing to the rain forests, what they're doing with bovine growth hormone, what they're spilling in our oceans," Freddie said.

"The repressive governments of Nigeria and Burma," Victor said.

"Amen," Freddie said.

"In a bottle," Winter said.

"Bad infant formula in developing countries," Victor said. "They kill millions."

"On the other hand, maybe not us," Freddie said.

Victor leaned forward and tapped a left-handed high-five with her. "Bonus round," he said. "You know how they make Premarin?"

"Pregnant mares," Winter and Freddie said together. "High school."

"Yeah. Me, too. Plus, I saw a thing on TV. Tiny stalls, no water or exercise, forced into pregnancy every year, then three months into it they're tied up in these stalls and this rubber collection cup sort of attached to capture the urine. They don't do anything but stand there and pee for months. The foals end up slaughtered for food for Asia."

The other two turned and stared. I stared in the rearview.

"Well? They do. I saw it," he said.

———

We took I-10 straight through, and it was an easy, quick drive. At Diamondhead I called Clare and told her where we were and that we'd be there in forty-five minutes. There wasn't much chatter after that. We all stared out our windows and thought the kinds of things you think in a car at eighty miles an hour when you finally get over the discomfort of too many people too close together for too long. The sun was still high behind us in the western sky when we curved off I-10 at Biloxi and made the loop at the D'Iberville exit.

"We're all going to your house?" Victor said.

"For the moment," I said. "It's not really my house any more, I mean—I don't live there. I mean, I have a financial interest in the house, of course, but..."

"Oh, shut up," Winter said.

"I have a place on the beach in Biloxi," I said.

"I live there some," Winter said.

"Maybe you should run us over to my place," Freddie said. "Victor can stay with me, you and Winter can go to your house."

"Already there," I said.

I circled under the overpass and drove the narrow road out to the house on Back Bay. We skirted the water for a mile or so, and then I steered the car up the long curved oyster-shell drive-way, overgrown on both sides with thick foliage, bamboo, pines, palms, and hanging vines that swept across the windshield of the car. The house wasn't visible from the street or the drive. It was nice—looked more like Florida than Mississippi.

Freddie's head tilted against the passenger window. Winter sat up, leaning on the backs of the two front seats, staring out the front windshield.

"So this is where you all come from," Victor said.

Winter said, "Some of the stuff that grows around here would surprise you."

Victor did mock-surprise—raised his eyebrows, dropped his jaw, and then slid back into his seat. "Whatever," he said.

Freddie turned and looked over the seat at him. "She just meant that we're home," Freddie said.

"Yes, ma'am," he said. "I got that."

I stopped in front of the house. The live oaks were draped with moss, the tall pines swayed, the deep front porch stretched across the facade. We got out and stood alongside the car as if we were ready for a group portrait.

21

I was nervous about being back and staying at the house, but it seemed too difficult to drive around and drop everybody off all over town. After the long drive, the others had misgivings about staying at Clare's. Winter and Victor had to have a talk. Freddie wanted to call a cab and get back to her place. It was a mess there for a bit, and it took a while to get everybody settled. But eventually we got the rooms assigned, the baths figured out, and then we retired to our various rooms. This was usually my favorite part of the trip—being done with it, finished with the traveling, even temporarily. That moment in some strange room where everything is *other*—you are not responsible, you don't own it, you don't have to look after it, and you are free to ignore it. It isn't your room, after all. And it's wonderful that the lamps and rugs aren't yours, and that they can't claw at you, remind you of things you'd rather not be reminded of.

That wasn't quite true for me this time, but I was in one of the guest bedrooms, and it was strange enough. I lay on the bed and shut my eyes, thinking that nobody really likes marriage, that it's a flawed arrangement, that people get enthusiastic and jump in for a hundred reasons and then, after the ceremony, after a few years, the whole deal turns into a concert they wouldn't have dreamed of attending.

I always figured Clare never quite loved me anyway. I was some dime store art teacher. A clean guy, but a guy with no real prospects. I told her this one night, years after we were married, and she just kind of waved the idea away as if it were nonsense, but I could tell that it was too close for comfort. Later she said she didn't know about love in the first place, that marriage was a math problem you don't ever get the answer to.

That didn't seem wrong to me. People get together and they stay together, Lord knows why. They wish for something else, maybe long for it, but eventually they shrug it off and go out to work in the garden. It's worse now than in the old days, in my parents' time. They knew how to do marriage better than people now, and I suspect people before my parents knew how to do marriage better than they. Lower expectations, maybe that was it. Like a clean house and a warm meal—that pretty much did it. In my father's time, people believed in kindness the way nobody believes in kindness anymore.

My parents met in college in the '30s, moved to Florida where my father started a business. He did well, and they had children—me and my brother and sister. My parents liked each other pretty well, even through the hard times. After a while he sold the business and wrote for the newspaper.

I remember a house we lived in during the early '50s—a kind of sun-oriented thing, lots of glass looking out on a big lawn, lots of sunlight, a big overhang on the terrace, lots of flowers, lots of gravel in the flowerbeds in the yard. I remember strange-looking swimsuits, inner tubes we took to the beach south of Tallahassee, eight-millimeter movies my father made of Mother and the children in the water. The air in those days was lighter than the air we get these days. The sun was crisper. The nights were sweeter. The lightning bugs brighter.

My mother and father were like curators of our little museum—the museum that was our house and our family and the way we lived. They each had *interests* in the evenings. One would be reading a magazine in one room, and the other would be in another room with a book. We would run from one to the other asking this and that. They would stop and occasionally one would yell to the other, sending one of us kids with a question. And then, after a time, everybody got up and stretched and met up in the kitchen for snacks—leftovers from the refrigerator.

We kids had a whole life built around them, built around the world they lived in, the values they had, the way they talked about other people and about what they were doing, the way we kept our house and cleaned our rooms and did our schoolwork.

We got all that from them. Schoolwork was fun. Schoolwork was interesting, sometimes challenging, always doable. It was an Ozzie and Harriet thing. My father covered city politics, state politics, and in his spare time he wrote about architecture and painting and theater. He was kind of an odd bird for Tallahassee in the '40s and '50s. My mother taught school for a while. She was handsome and sweet and patient with the children, and we all adored her.

Sometimes I thought that getting the condominium after Clare and I split, living there on the beach, keeping it simple, I was getting back to something my parents had when I was a kid. Some natural order, where simple things like modest breezes and pale moonlight could make you feel as if you were O.K., make you feel that the world was a sufficient place.

I didn't know how they had handled all the crap that goes through your mind. Maybe they didn't have so much. They didn't have television screeching at them all the time. They didn't have the same magazines, the same crappy movies. They had radio. And maybe everyone was more generous then. It may have been easier to be generous, because the people you were generous to were generous right back. Anyway, that's the way it seemed. I was this kid in this little spaceship my parents made, and that's the way it was in there.

I think I loved my parents more than was healthy. That has stuck with me over the years, long after their deaths, so that I still have this feeling for them. Not like I had when they were older and I was an adult, but like I had when I was a kid, when they were young themselves. The pleasures in the world seemed clearer and more intense. I remember loving pencils. I was fond of paper. I loved the smell of textbooks. I loved the way the light from a desk lamp was bright on a page. I loved the smell of fresh-cut grass. It was a thing everybody loved, but there was no shame in being that much like everybody else, in sharing that. I loved the deadened slow motion of summer afternoons without a cloud in the sky. The company of other kids. I had friends when I was ten. I loved window screens. And the smell when you opened windows. And the pile of an area rug underfoot. And the scent of my mother's clothes. I loved the gritty feel of my father's chin, the way his eyes looked behind his rimless glasses, shining and strong, and the sound of his footsteps on the polished hardwood floors as he went to the hall mirror to tie his tie each morning. I loved his starched white shirts.

22

Eventually everybody started coming down to the kitchen. We'd already decided we were going out for dinner, but everyone seemed to want to be in the kitchen anyway. Victor was messing with the vacuum sealer and a plastic bag of tomatoes. Winter was playing with the dog. Freddie was arranging fruit in the wooden bowl.

"Jesus, what's that arm like?" Clare said, pointing to Freddie's injury.

"It's not that bad, really. Sore, you know? But kind of interesting."

"Hmm," Clare said. "She's your kind of girl, Elroy."

I rolled my eyes. Clare rolled hers right back.

Victor turned on the sealer. "You got anything that needs sealing? Man, I just want to seal everything in sight. I want to seal that Microsoft mouse," he said, pointing at the computer.

"How long before it heals?" Clare said.

"Couple of weeks. Then I'll have a scar."

"The men love scars," Clare said. She crossed the kitchen to get bowls, put them on the counter, then straightened up, brushing both palms back over her hair.

"No," Winter said, whacking a tomato. "They really don't. Just my opinion."

"O.K.," Clare said. "I'm just glad you guys are back. It's dull without you here, you know?" She looked at Winter, then me.

Winter got up and pulled Wavy out of the room. "C'mon, Victor. I'll show you the layout while there's still plenty of light," she said.

He rinsed his hands in the sink, dried them on a dishcloth, followed her out.

"So?" Clare said.

"I'm glad to be back," I said. "The trip was, you know, like, nuts."

"We didn't know what the deal was," Freddie said. "From the minute we arrived in Memphis we were kind of lost."

"Victor didn't expect all of us to come get him," I said.

"I guessed that," Clare said.

Outside the kitchen window Victor and Winter went by on the covered walkway, headed for the carriage house.

"Let's sit down a minute," Clare said. She took Freddie's arm and led her into the small sitting room off the kitchen, a room Clare used all the time. Clare sat in the rocker.

Freddie started to light up. Clare plucked the cigarette from her mouth, examined the cigarette, and placed it unlit on the coffee table. "Elroy's a decent man," she said. "Fair, honest. Smart—you're smart, aren't you, Elroy?"

"Not anymore," I said.

Clare rolled the cigarette around on the table, then picked it up, put it in her mouth, motioned for a light.

"You don't want that," I said.

"I do. I want it exactly."

She lit the cigarette and drew the smoke into her lungs. "So, Freddie, you want to explain to me again how you've had this really hard life, brutalized by foster parents, traveling around, nowhere to go—you want to run that by me again?"

Freddie looked at Clare, expressionless, the way kids do it. Blank. Perfectly calm, no facial feature disturbed.

I said, "Do we want to do this now, Clare? I mean, why do we want to do this right now?"

Clare stubbed the cigarette out in a big ashtray. "Because, sweetheart."

Freddie's perfect expression started to fade. She looked sad, lost. Caught. On the TV in the background some children were playing on a mound of garbage. We sat like that for a moment, the TV going, no one speaking. Then Clare leaned over and patted

Freddie's hair, traced a finger down the edge of Freddie's jaw. "It's all right, dear," Clare said, waving her hand dismissively. "I just needed to see a little something from you."

We went to Captain Sugar's Fish House, a decaying restaurant stuck up on pilings at the edge of a pier at the east end of Biloxi. The white walls were plastered with ancient photos, Biloxi in the early 1900s, boat building, and men in hats. The tables were spotless—linen tablecloths, heavy old silverware, gardenias in crystal clear water. Out the windows, spotlights hit the pier and the Gulf. We all crowded around a corner table. The windows were cranked open, and you could smell the salt water, hear it slapping at pilings, hear the thud of boats bumping the pier.

"I'm not hungry," Freddie said, fooling with her knife, banging it into her spoon.

"O.K., what's the deal?" Winter said. "Were you and Mom talking? Mom, did you talk to her?"

"Sure. Of course," Clare said.

I wagged a finger. "Let's settle down and have a nice dinner."

"Elroy has the right idea," Clare said. "We're in a complicated situation. We can't pretend the obvious stuff is the only stuff."

"So what'd you guys say?" Winter said.

Then Victor, in what seemed to me a generous gesture, put an arm around Winter's shoulder and asked her about things he pointed to out the window—the marina, the boats.

"How's the calamari?" Freddie said.

"Rubbery and tasteless. You'll love it," Clare said. When everybody turned to look at her, she said, "It's an old joke. Elroy and I had this joke many years ago. I'm reprising it here today."

"This is true," I said. "In the days when she ate squid and I did not. But now—now I eat squid at every meal!"

Clare grinned at Freddie. "Usually it's good," she said. "Excellent. Order. I'll have some, too."

"I'm having fried chicken," Victor said. "When I was a kid, I always had fried chicken at the seafood joints when we went to the beach."

We studied our menus, then ordered when the skinny bucktoothed waitress arrived. After that we sat there staring out the windows at the Gulf.

Winter said, "So, when we were checking out this morning, Victor got in this argument with that huge guy behind the counter, you know?"

"The Bayside Sleeper," I said to Clare. "Outside of Lafayette."

"The place was all plate glass and bamboo shades and a fish tank with that one giant fish."

"We didn't watch any movies," Victor said.

"Right," she said. "But he was saying we had. I told him no, no movies, and he said, 'Says right here you watched *Catamaran Queens* for four minutes.' So I said, 'Maybe we hit it accidentally, but we didn't watch it. Four minutes isn't watching it.'"

"So he flaps his paper around," Victor said, "like he's swatting flies."

"He shrugged enormously," Winter said. "Told us that he'd seen a lot since he bought the motel and that rules were rules. They were printed right there on the television sets: over two minutes you get charged for the whole movie."

"There's a reason for everything, he told us," Victor said.

"O.K.," Clare said. "What's the reason?"

"So the guy says, 'I guess you don't read *The Journal of the American Medical Association,* huh?'" Victor said, grinning.

Clare paused, then nodded. "I see," she said.

It seemed like nothing was going to work, but the rest of dinner was comparatively quiet, uneventful. We took turns filling Clare in on the trip; Victor told us all about his time with Furlong and apologized for getting everybody into the mess to start with.

"I just liked Winter, is all," he said. "She seemed terrific, and I thought it would be fun to, you know, see Memphis with her, that kind of thing." He was obviously embarrassed but what stunned me was how comfortable he was with it. Somehow putting Clare into the equation completely mellowed him out, and he was just this nice kid for a while. I started wondering if he was staying around or heading out again, thinking maybe he'd be good for Winter in the long term, a stabilizing influence.

So the dinner turned out fine. There was conversation and there were jokes and the food was good, and pretty soon everybody seemed comfortable in a way that I couldn't have imagined a couple of hours earlier.

After dinner the others walked out to the end of the pier. Freddie and I were left to talk. I asked if she was doing O.K.

"Why wouldn't I be, El?"

"Who knows? Maybe I ran out of luck or something."

"I don't think so. I think you've got all the luck in the world. And then some."

This put me on edge. Something new had crept in, some change had happened, and I hadn't actually recognized it. I wasn't surprised that it was there in Freddie's voice, but I wasn't ready for it, either. "Maybe I shouldn't talk? I should just stand here and be one hundred percent mute?"

"Has potential," she said.

I stared at her and leaned back in my chair. Out the window Winter rested against a light pole, while Victor and Clare sat on the edge of the pier, dangling their feet over the dark sparkling Gulf.

We went outside and sat with them, listening to the lap of waves against the pier, the hiss and rattle of water running around the pilings. Clare moved over to lean against a rough wooden rail.

"You're a lot like Freddie," Victor said to her.

Clare looked at Victor for a minute, then broke down and smiled, looking out over the water. "Who taught you to do that?" she said.

Victor said, "Wasn't thinking."

"You haven't been in town long, right?" Clare said.

"Right. Furlong got me off a highway outside of Carlsbad a few years ago, and we've been pals ever since," he said. "Then I came here and ran into your daughter."

"The rest is history," Winter said. "That's what he says."

Out in the Gulf, a low-hulled boat chugged by, glittering with lights. All of us watched and listened. "Love's a puzzle, isn't it?" Clare said.

"Well, yeah," Victor said. "Sure. But, you know, after a while, I mean, I'm trying not to push things—"

Winter slapped his arm. "Don't be so talky," she said.

"I'm not being talky. I'm just being—"Victor froze a second, and then they both laughed. "I guess I am, huh?"

Winter tapped Victor's shoulder again and got up, stamping her feet on the pier. "Who wants to walk?"

"Me," Clare said.

———

Nobody wanted to split up the group, so we stayed at the house for a few days, sort of like we were on vacation, as if we were a bunch of friends who had gotten together for some time at the beach.

One late morning three of us were on the stone terrace by the carriage house. The terrace was sprinkled with sunlight that cut through the umbrella of limbs and leaves above.

"We could just take off now," Victor said. "Cut the cord. We got Mr. Big back here, so we're free to go, right?"

Freddie hooked an arm in Victor's arm. "We could do that, Victor. Yes."

"I remind you that we're going out in the boat this afternoon," I said. "Besides, I'm looking for both of you guys to stay in town. Freddie's got to go back to school."

Now she patted *my* arm. "We'll see, El. I may want a rain check on that after all. But Winter and Victor have other interests. He's, uh, how shall I say this? Taken? Taken with her?"

"I observed as much," I said. "And she does not have a single communicable disease, she is not HIV positive, she is not a junkie, she does not believe she has been cruelly treated by everyone she ever met—why, she's fresh air in this world!"

"Unlike who, exactly?" Freddie said, tightening her grip on my arm.

"I was speaking broadly about our cultural fascination with trouble."

"You were?"

"Yes, our inclination to equate trouble with meaning, like the idea that a junkie, for example, is interesting. By definition. I mean, could it be that a junkie is simply dumb as dirt? *Sacre bleu!*"

"He doesn't like junkies?" Victor said.

"I don't like people who brag about their hard times," I said.

"He's a tough room," Victor said.

Freddie shrugged. "A pet peeve, I think." We sat on the ledge beside the small pond. Goldfish swam.

Later that same day the five of us headed out into the Gulf, with me at the helm of a twenty-three-foot, center-console Grady White that belonged to a friend of ours. I had a big dollop of zinc ointment meringued up over my nose.

"You look like what's-his-name in that movie where he had the metal nose," Freddie said.

"Lee Marvin," Clare said.

"Isn't he dead?" Winter said.

"Who?" I said.

When we were out far enough, I pushed the throttle forward and brought the boat up on plane. Victor and Winter were at the front and got assaulted with spray thrown off the bow. They hung onto the chrome rail, their hair blown straight back.

Freddie sat in one of the two cockpit chairs alongside Clare. I was just in front of them. Clare leaned forward and shouted into my ear. "Tell me that everything is going to be all right. Tell me that the worst is over."

I pointed at Deer Island like I was showing her the sites. I pointed back toward the beach where you could make out the Windswept Condominiums.

Clare nodded and smiled tightly, her skin radiant with the afternoon sun.

After a bit I brought the boat back down and gave the wheel to Clare, stood alongside the console under the T-top.

"How about this, huh? Is this perfect, or what?" I said.

Clare smiled. "It's not bad, Elroy."

We were out for a few hours, long enough for everybody to get a little bit crabby and burned. Late in the afternoon I eased the boat into its slip. A few water-stained power boats were tied up on either side.

We were all on wobbly legs, our hair smeared back. We looked wind-blistered, blown, salty. I busied myself with ropes while the rest were hopping to get off the boat.

Freddie went up the gray wooden pier by herself.

23

———

At the house that night I went to Freddie's room. Freddie was in the bath, and I tapped on the door, and when she didn't answer, I opened the door and stepped in. She was in clear water up to her chin. Her eyes were closed. She was completely out of this world.

She reached for a towel, found only a bath cloth, which she draped over her breasts. "Get out, Elroy. C'mon. Not here, for Christ's sake."

"I need to talk."

"Not now," she said. "Just get out."

She got out of the tub. The cloth fell away. She grabbed a bottle of shampoo and threw it, caught me on the side of the head.

"Now," she said. "I'm throwing things until you go."

She picked up a ceramic soap dish and threw that at me. It hit me on the shoulder. She was close to me now.

I struggled to get out of the bathroom but was too close to the door and hit myself with it. "I'm going, trying to go," I said.

I shoved her back, my hand on her bare wet shoulder, so that I could clear the door. She slipped and fell against the lavatory.

"Fuck," she said. "God damn it, Elroy."

I started to come back into the bathroom to help her, but she wagged her head and gave me the finger, shook it at me. Vehemence.

I stopped in the door and then reached for the knob, but her foot was in the way so I couldn't close it. I stood there for a minute, watching her. She stayed down. After a second she lay back on the bathroom floor in an awkwardly twisted position, her cheek pressed against the cold tile, her eyes looking straight ahead. Water pooled on the tile.

I backed out of the room and went downstairs.

———

An hour later I came back. I knocked on the bedroom door and then went in. Winter and Freddie were on the bed together, sitting up against the headboard. They drank something hot out of coffee mugs. Across the room, a talk-show host was on television with his panel of talking heads. Pictures of stolen girls were inset into the screen behind him.

"Change it, will you? Find *Animal Planet*," Freddie said.

"I expected to be there by now," Winter said, flipping the channels.

"It's sixty-something," Freddie said.

"Victor seems pretty nice after all," I said.

"I think he is becoming some kind of a religious nut," Winter said. She waved the remote and kept punching keys.

"That wouldn't hurt, "I said. "We could use some of that around here."

"I don't think it'll last," Freddie said.

Winter got off the bed, kissed Freddie on the cheek, headed for the door. "I'm going downstairs."

"Hang on," Freddie said, pushing off the bed. "We're coming, too."

We went down to the sitting room, where Victor and Clare were having coffee and cookies. They were watching the same talk show that was on upstairs. Winter picked up a cookie and glanced at the TV. "This is not good for my morale," she said.

"Where've you guys been?" Victor said.

"Upstairs," Freddie said. "Watching *Animal Planet*. I'm at my best watching *Animal Planet*."

"We all are," Clare said.

"Something, something, soothes the something of the Spanish beast," Victor said.

Clare looked at him, looked at the television, then back at him. "Switch it," she said, getting up. "Show these women what they want to see."

She left the room and went out the back door. I followed her, found her leaning against a white-painted column on the breeze-way, her temple against the wood. She moved slightly against the post, started walking toward the carriage house. Her movements were musical; she was almost dancing.

"What're we doing now?" I said.

"Let's take a break, Elroy," she said. "Just you and me. Together. They can entertain each other, can't they?"

"Sure," I said.

In the carriage house she slid a video into the VCR, and we sat on the old couch in front of the large television. In a minute the room was filled with funky Mexican cantina music, and on the screen a young Winter danced in circles on the patio of a desert motel. Clare had the remote in one hand, ticking it at the screen in time with the music.

We watched this for a few minutes, and then Clare looked out the French doors at the pond on the terrace. She got up and circled the room until she was directly behind me. She looked at the television screen—Winter dancing.

"She was so lovely that summer," Clare said.

"She was that," I said.

Clare bent over me, ran her hands down my arms, kissed my cheek, wedged the remote into my hand, stayed that way for a long second or two, then stood up. I lowered the volume, exam-ined the remote as if it were a thing from some other world, something I'd never seen before.

"I've always wondered what this would be like," she said. "A house full of people." She made a handgun out of her hand and pretended to shoot me in the temple.

"Clare."

"Hush, Elroy." She drew a heart on my skull with her gun finger.

I reached up and grabbed the finger, gave it a little tug. She stood behind me, pulling away.

We watched this home video of Winter outside an Indian Chief motel some holiday season ten or twelve years before. She was a young and lovely child wearing a thin white nightgown, twirling in time with this haunting music. Behind her the sun settled into the dust of that desert summer.

24

I ran Victor and Freddie out to her place the next afternoon, leaving Winter with her mother. I got to Windswept about four and slept right through the evening and then woke up at ten and bathed.

Gretchen and Mrs. Scree arrived while I was still drying my hair. "How was the trip?" Mrs. Scree wanted to know.

"Aren't you guys up a little late?" I said.

"We're party girls," Gretchen said. She looked slick as ever, toned up, fit, with a well-done tanning-bed tan.

I offered them coffee; they took beer. I went to the bedroom to put on a better shirt and stopped for a second in the bathroom to see what I looked like, came away disappointed, as usual.

We sat at the dining table, and I reported on the trip. They listened impatiently, so I cut it short.

Mrs. Scree said things were getting back to normal and that this had been a very difficult period for all of us.

"Amen to that," I said.

"No question," Gretchen said.

"The worst," Mrs. Scree said.

Then Gretchen started talking about a billboard a block down from Windswept Condominiums. "It's Budweiser," she said. "You've got to see it. It's all about sex. This girl serving beer, young girl—"

"All of them are," Mrs. Scree said, making a face at me.

"So she's like on the left end of the billboard, leaning into the, you know—the board, the space—and she's just at this certain angle, a pretty blond."

"Naturally," Mrs. Scree said.

"Can I smoke in here?" Gretchen said, pulling out her cigarette case.

"Not supposed to," I said.

Gretchen smiled at me then, as I suspect she had smiled at others before, husbands, boyfriends, colleagues, coworkers, lovers, her perfectly white actor's teeth porcelain bright. "So she's up there and she's wearing this T-shirt that makes her breasts incredibly sensual," Gretchen said. "You can almost *feel* the weight of them from the street."

"Here we go," Mrs. Scree said. She pulled a cigarette out of Gretchen's case and rolled it between her lips.

"Oh, hush, Eleanor," Gretchen said.

"You're getting to be a prude, dear," Mrs. Scree said. She lit up and took a deep drag and then let the smoke roll out on either side of the filter.

"It pisses me off," Gretchen said. "You *know* they're all thrilled to have this woman's tits pressing against the fabric, heavy, soft—"

"All right, that's it for me," Mrs. Scree said, getting out of her chair.

I tried to smile without getting my lips tangled up in my teeth.

"I just wonder if everybody notices the insistent sexuality of this woman's breasts as she's serving this guy his beer," Gretchen said. "That's all."

I leaned forward and caught her hand in mine, turned it to look at her palm. "I can help you with that," I said. "Yes."

She stopped then. I felt her hand holding onto mine, a tiny pressure that lasted just a few seconds, as if she'd suddenly seen the whole picture of the three of us up there at midnight in my empty flat. She nodded, and said, "Good. Thanks, that's helpful. I feel better now with that . . . settled. But really, take a look next time you leave the building. It's something."

"I will take a look," I said.

We got quiet a minute, and I realized I'd better do something, so I asked again why she and Mrs. Scree were up so late.

"Waiting for you, I guess," Mrs. Scree said. "Would you believe that?"

Gretchen dug lightly at my wrist with her fingernail.

"Wouldn't it be lovely," I said. It was supposed to sound off-hand, like a politely appreciative joke, but there was too much spin on it.

"Stranger things," she said.

———

They left shortly after eleven, after I promised to come over the next day and see Mrs. Scree's new pet fish, some kind of special fish she had gotten from the pet store, and after Gretchen and I exchanged assurances about getting together for dinner very soon.

When they were gone I cleaned up and trashed the beer bottles, then went out to sit for a few minutes on the balcony. The night was lovely, clear, with cotton-white clouds streaming past a full moon.

I got the Nikon digital and took a few photographs of the moon high in the sky. It was still early, or relatively early, and it was a pleasure to be outside. The moon was intense, insistent, like a night sun, but spreading that creamier light, cool and soft, shadowy, as if it were teenage shy.

Standing at the rail I could survey the balconies of the other units in my building, sometimes the rooms beyond, my neighbors in various states of disarray, the way we all are at home. For years I wanted to catch women undressed looking in windows, but I did once or twice, in various places where Clare and I lived, and it was—how shall I characterize this?—it was unsatisfying. The women were less beautiful undressed than they were dressed. Less mysterious and compelling, less alluring, less interesting. They were like slightly wounded animals, which is what I imagine we all are in our private moments, thrown across a couch or slouched in a chair, half in and half out of bed, going to the kitchen to fetch snacks during the commercials. It was an awful realization and of course I knew beforehand, but I had never *seen*. So after that I was less interested in spying on women, naked women, or in seeing anyone at all, and more aware that people play with themselves a great deal. I believe we adjust our parts, fiddle with our noses and ears, scratch ourselves every bit as much as dogs or cats. More than cats, perhaps.

———

I went inside and made myself a pretty drink in a heavy glass and took it out on the balcony, thinking that this would be a good time to spend a few minutes with the late Edward Works, discussing all that had transpired. I wanted to imagine what he might have said if I'd caught him the night he died. I'd have started with "What're you up to?" and he'd have replied, "Nothing." Then awkwardness, circling in his apartment, my first visit there, the place a mirror of mine, perhaps—no furniture, the sparest of appointments, the living room a small gallery for Edward's works. I'd admire them, walk around the room, nodding in front of pieces, smiling, laughing when the work was particularly charming. He'd watch me. He'd be in the kitchen, standing behind the pass-through, his hands on the countertop. "You're very good," I'd say. "I'm proud of you and all this work." He'd thank me in a matter-of-fact way. The awkwardness would persist. I'd stand at his window, looking north over the back of Biloxi, out toward Keesler and Back Bay. Clare's house. "You're not supposed to fuck the students," he'd say. Or maybe he wouldn't say that at all, maybe that's me. I'd want to explain something to him, something about being older and being tired and being cut off from things, feeling cut off, feeling as if you had once mattered and then something happened and you didn't matter anymore—not to your wife, your friends, your colleagues, other painters, anybody. Sort of tell him how it works—maybe that's what I would have done, though what I wonder is how that would have helped him. What would have stopped him? I could have explained that we were all the same, that he and I were just like everybody else, that *everybody* was like everybody else, that it was remarkable how alike we all were. But I couldn't figure out why that would make him want to live, want to go on. I thought it might ease his mind, take some pressure off, if he didn't think he had everything hanging in the balance on every play, if he could take some days off, if we all shared something, if we were all in it together in some way that wasn't readily apparent in ordinary life. I was thinking this might ease his mind.

I looked at the drink in my hand and then held it up against the moonlit sky. Clouds ran through it. I wanted to say to Edward that I was sorry he was gone, that we were all so sorry he was gone. We were out here standing around looking for him, waiting for him. We were doing our jobs, climbing into our little holes at night, but we missed him terribly.

I would have told Edward that there are some things you regret forever. There was a girl in high school. We were not going to make it to intimacy, or even much past friendship. We longed for each other, I think, the two of us, until I ruined even that. I was seventeen; she was Mexican. I was a middle-class white boy—nice clothes, nice family, nice car. She worked at the A&W and went to Sacred Heart High School. I liked her a good deal. She was smart and funny, pretty, a pleasure to be with. We got closer, but then I began backing away, *because* she was Mexican. I don't know how this happened, why this bothered me, but after two months I told her I couldn't see her anymore. I took her downtown in my mother's Lincoln, and we sat on a landscaped hill next to an old hotel in a lovely light-spattered lay of grass surrounded by concrete, and I told her I couldn't see her anymore because she was Mexican. I don't know why I had to tell her, why I even had the thought, and I still wish there were some forgiving circumstance, but I do not think that there was. I wish I could say that it wasn't so bad, that I was a kid, that it didn't matter. But it did. She has haunted my dreams ever since.

So there's that one. I could've told him that story and maybe slowed him down. Or maybe I could have told him about Winter, about my regrets there; I hadn't been a father, not even a stepfather. I was just this guy her mother had been living with for years.

I wouldn't ever have made it in the father business. Maybe if she had been my child, if I'd ever felt she was mine, then I could have done better. Lord knows lots of mugs get to be fathers, and maybe I could have risen to the occasion. But I hadn't, so Winter had always been just like another smaller woman to me. And that was trouble, because she was pretty and young and had all that good skin, and every second thought I had about her had this sexual edge I couldn't quite dodge—looking down her shirt, looking at her butt in her tight jeans, patting her bare back just to feel her skin. Creepy. She was like a walking advertisement for great sex with children. Nothing happened, but I always wondered. The truth was that as a father, or just another human, I couldn't get her to take me seriously, so that I might have had a chance to say something meaningful to her, to be a part of her life. We were strays from opposite ends of the age curve who didn't get along, and we were living in the same shed. After a couple shots at fatherly advice that she sat through with log-like indifference, I gave up, and after that I lost patience. I made fun of her, I avoided her, I shrugged whenever it was my turn to have some opinion. Clare and I tried to talk about her, but that went badly too, and eventually we gave that up as well. On a one to ten scale, I was maybe a one. If you were counting hard.

I wanted Edward Works to study these regrets. To avoid them for himself. To remember that all you really want is some new turf to inhabit and somebody to see it with, to stare at the television of day-to-day life with, quiet, in the same room, side by side on a sofa.

So it was coming to me that everything I might have had to say to Edward on the night of his demise was all about me, my regrets, my anticipated pleasures, the animals buried in my yard, the clothes in my closet, the little tin fireplace in which I burned Duraflame New "Crackling" Firelogs that I bought at the grocery store. When I wanted to say something about art, about what it is to spend a lifetime doing it not all that well, being neither the iconoclast oblivious to everything but the art, nor the careerist, constantly bending the art to fit comfortably the glove of culture, it dawned on me that he might not have the same problems.

My drink was watery. A life-flight helicopter swept overhead, swung out over the water, its blades thucking like the choppers in a Vietnam movie. The pilot swiveled around as if facing me, bright lights in my eyes, then tilted off westward, toward the medical center. I went inside.

What was the message I failed to get to Edward Works in time? It was something about *other people,* wasn't it? That they counted. That being a bad-ass artist who later in life settles down to become a solid citizen, a professor of art, a respected *practitioner* of art is not enough, not nearly enough, and that Edward had to stop and reflect on his inescapable kinship with *other people,* all the ones who were still alive, all the people he did not particularly like, who looked or smelled peculiar to him, who had more hair or less hair, better wives or lesser wives, better condos or lesser ones, cars, animals, charge cards the same as his, who walked different ways but went to the same places, who told different jokes that were the same jokes. All those people. They went to the same restaurants! Ate what he ate, shopped at the same malls, the same stores, went to the same Blockbuster where they rented the same movies—there was something wholesome and terrifying about what he shared with others.

I would have advised Edward to watch the people on television to see what all of us are like now, to see how we are getting along. He should watch us being interviewed on the news programs, on Jay Leno, on the midday talk show on CNN, where the stub-nosed woman has a little audience up in little bleachers, and some issue is discussed, and people in the audience—*us!*—offered tiny opinions, just like ours, just like the ratty TV talkers, only smaller in scale. Just the fact that we were out there in all those condominiums and houses and apartments, high-rises on the beach in Florida and Texas and California, watching each other, was an enormously satisfying thing. I would have explained to Edward that we were in good hands.

Sometimes you will feel a little slighted, I would have told him. As if others are not giving you the credit you are giving them. It's an odd feeling.

At a stoplight, when I am waiting alongside another car, I might look over at the driver next to me. He looks back at me and, just before he turns away, an expression crosses his face that suggests that I do not matter, as if he does not recognize me as being like him at all, as if he is looking at me and thinking, *"Who's this fool?"* just as he turns away. There is some little pouty expression on his face, some little blink of the eye, some dismissive gesture—the way he tosses his hair back, the way he reaches for the radio in his way-too-expensive sixty-month lease, the way he holds his cigarette—when we both know we are the same person, after all is said and done. I want to get out of the car then, walk over to the guy, yank on his door handle, and pull him out of that plush leather seat, pull him out into the middle of the road and say hello, shake his stupid hand. Tell him that he's got me worried, that when I see him, I get upset. Remind him about all those dirty little people we see on television at night, people in foreign countries on television in their strange little houses with their strange little wood tables and their grass mats and dirt floors and homemade chairs, tell this fool in the intersection that when I see these people padding around in their dirt streets and in their huts in their bare feet, the soles of their feet white with dust, when they sit cross-legged facing the camera, I wonder if *they* aren't also just like us. Don't those men look at the women in their villages and wish they could have those women? Don't they look at the big Range Rovers that drive through and wish they could have those cars? And I would tell Edward that I'd tell the guy I've pulled out of the car that yes, those people are exactly like us, too. And see there? They are not mocking others at stoplights, they are not putting on airs or showing a lot more attitude than necessary, they are not jumping out of their huts and killing themselves, and that should be the first lesson for us all—*restraint.* And the second lesson is: *We are monkeys.*

25

Sometime after Freddie went back out to Santa Fe, I started spending a lot of time late at night at Clare's house on the bay, sitting out there on her deck in the middle of the night. She caught me once, and it frightened her, but after that I think it was comforting to her that I came over so often, just to spend time sitting out there while she slept. It was always two or three in the morning, clouds slowly drifting west, the lights from across the bay reflected in the water, streaks of gold and blue, water textured like shiny pudding. I felt mosquitoes walking on my arms, kept brushing them off. Then a timid breeze would come like a blanket, a light, fresh blanket, covering my legs, my arms, my face. I would sit and listen to the sounds of the night—crickets, cars and trucks on the highway, an occasional cat's meow, a dog barking, birds yakking in the little stand of woods at the edge of the property. Sometimes I'd just close my eyes and try to be a stereo receiver, calculating the stereo image in my mind, hearing the whine of a jet off to the right somewhere behind me, a couple of cars passing on the road in front of the house. Off to the left in the distance a big truck shifting up through the gears as it went out on Highway 24. More cars. The light lap of the water at the bulkhead. In the extreme distance to the right at about two o'clock some diesel sound. The sound of a bird squeaking somewhere across the water, low, and throaty frogs calling and responding. The air-conditioning compressor kicking on, rattling. These were the loveliest times for me because they were the times I knew that everyone was safe. Clare was. Winter was. I was.

The clouds going by were like massive armies on a silent march, off to do battle with some other force, some other place, and the whole sky was a Japanese war poem. I wondered how many people had stared at clouds for how many years in history. How many people had spent nights just like mine, watching the clouds go by at three in the morning? It was astonishing to think that people around the world did this exact thing. It reminded me of the postcard about all the people in China jumping off the ground at the same time in the hope of throwing the earth out of orbit.

Safety is a condition we all seek. But it doesn't mean what it used to mean. Now it's temporary, a Just Visiting slot outside the jail. A place you can stay a few hours and with some confidence predict that the world will not collapse around your ears. Most of my confidence comes from the fact that it's three in the morning and people are asleep, and I figure they are not going to fuck up while they are asleep. This gives me rest, room to breathe, a chance to think about what's going on in my life—what I'm going to do about teaching, what I'm going to do about Clare, what I might have done about Freddie. The world is full of stories, movies, books, plays, television shows, for God's sake, about men who fall for tiny women, women who are barely women at all, barely more than girls. We love our girls, walking around in their short pants and tank tops, all ready to be instructed. We can't resist their charms, the sweet unfettered look of them, the naïveté, or the fresh, self-conscious guile. The culture is filled with these stories, and I had lived it exactly, the usual tortured fantasy of taking her away on a trip to a foreign place and becoming new to her, a complete person, not her teacher, not an older guy whose life is all but done, but a fresh man in whom she might be interested. I surprise myself with my own naïveté.

Clare has remained very patient on this point—my infatuations. I expected her to be angry. I believe she thinks it's funny, maybe pathetic. She screwed up her face once and said to me, "Elroy, you're not even a man to her. Can you imagine she looks at you and sees a lover?"

Because it was true, or because what Clare said hurt so much, I replied that Freddie *had* seen me as a lover.

This was crushing, of course. Clare smiled prettily, in a friendly way, and shook her head as if she had heard everything. It was defensive condescension. It was restrained, matter-of-fact.

I immediately apologized.

Clare smiled, nodded, and said she accepted my apology. And then she was all affection and kindness and sympathy. She was empathetic. She understood. She was steady.

I'd been seeing a woman half her age, a woman the age of her child, and Clare just rolled with the punch. She cared for me, thought of us as connected but not limited. She saw everything from her own view, and from a point of view not her own. Lip service is given to this, but I think this quality is rare.

So in the spring, on nights I went to Clare's and sat in the white wicker rocker with my feet on the white wooden rail, looking across the bay at the church, at the other houses, at the reflected lights on the water, I realized not only that I loved Clare, but that I had no other feeling for her, that we'd been together so long, been through so many things, done so much, been so many places, that we cared enough for each other that all that was left was love, this blanket of affection. I thought it was a love not often achieved.

———

In the first weeks and months of my return to the classroom, I could not give up looking at the young women in my charge, could not forego engaging them in some silly banter in the hall for the pure pleasure of staring at their faces, watching their eyes glitter. I loved to stare at them in the painting studio, at their tiny clothes, their fresh smooth skin, the smallness of their faces, the eagerness there, the seriousness. They thought that they were complete humans, full adults operating independently in the world, facing the world's large troubles with their art, seeing the world in a constantly new way, and I savored these young women.

When Victor turned up in my undergraduate painting class, I was surprised and thrilled. He had a palm-size digital camera, a Canon I believe it was, and he said he was going to take some pictures, blow them up at Kinko's, and write and draw on them. "That's just for starters," he said. "Winter showed me some of your stuff. It's pretty cool—some of those stories you put on there? Those sort of rock."

I thanked him for that and said I looked forward to seeing his pictures.

"I may do some computer stuff, too," he said. "I can do some stuff in Flash, or make DVDs or—I just don't know. I might do some animations."

He told me he had taken over Freddie's lease, that I should drop by sometime. I told him that I might do that.

The other male students were the usual assortment—loud-mouths and kids so shy they could barely speak above a whisper. I liked them all, found something interesting in their work always. People are interesting if you let them be. They were in the way, of course, these young men, taking time away from my female students, but I had time enough for all.

About the women, it occurred to me that there might be more far-reaching ways in which a mentor could help a student, that I might help them more thoroughly if I extended my relations with them, one after the other, in a wonderful series of endlessly careful instructions to them as individuals, thorough mentorships, some arrangement more elaborate than that of the strict, proper professor—the critic. I decided to take some time to reflect on that, to consider it fully.

So, while I went on living alone at Windswept Condominiums there on the beach in Biloxi, a place both austere and restful, where I no longer entertained my students, where I only occasionally brought Winter to watch a movie with me or have a half hour of machine-gun conversation, night after night I retired to the broad pine deck at Clare's house for quiet ruminations. I would roll up the long shadowy drive and leave my car in the circle in front of the house, go around the fence into the yard and come in under the deck, go quietly up the steps. I'd take one of the tired wicker chairs and place it directly at the top of the stairs and I'd sit, prop my feet on the railing, and smoke a few cigarettes, maybe have a drink, relishing the view. Sometimes Wavy padded up to the sliding door and saw me, scratched on the glass so that I would let him out; sometimes he just settled down inside and stared, full of expectation.